The Willows at Christmas

The Tales of the Willows

By Kenneth Grahame

The Wind in the Willows

By William Horwood

The Willows in Winter

Toad Triumphant

The Willows and Beyond

The Willows at Christmas

Also by William Horwood

The Duncton Wood series

The Stonor Eagles

Callanish

Skallagrigg

The Wolves of Time

WILLIAM HORWOOD

The Willows at Christmas

Illustrated by Patrick Benson

THOMAS DUNNE BOOKS
St. Martin's Press New York

THOMAS DUNNE BOOKS.
An imprint of St. Martin's Press.

www.stmartins.com

ISBN 0-312-28386-5

First published in Great Britain by
HarperCollins Publishers

First U.S. Edition: November 2001

10 9 8 7 6 5 4 3 2 1

Contents

·I·
Mr Mole Takes Action

"O my!" murmured Mr Mole of Mole End most unhappily as he stoked up his coal fire against the bitter December night. "O *dear*!"

There were only three days till Christmas Eve, but the Mole seemed to have quite lost all sense of seasonal excitement and good cheer. He traced his unwonted festive malaise directly back to a tea-time *tête à tête* he had had with his new friend Mr Toad of Toad Hall at the beginning of December.

Mole had been looking forward to this occasion with great anticipation. He had prepared well in advance, taking with him a greetings card he had made himself, as well as some of those festive sweetmeats he so expertly concocted in his kitchen. He was naturally a little surprised, therefore, that an unusually subdued Toad barely glanced at the card so lovingly made, and hardly picked at the sweetmeats.

The kind-hearted Mole put this down to there being something on the mind of Toad, whose changeable emotions, sudden enthusiasms and impulsive likes and dislikes were so well known along the River Bank. However, when a lull in the conversation prompted the Mole to produce his diary, so that he might discuss with his host his idea of entertaining their mutual friends Badger, Ratty and Otter to a festive celebration at Mole End, with Toad as guest of honour, an alarming change overtook Toad.

He frowned, shook his head, folded his arms across his chest and declared, "Absolutely impossible! I *never* accept engagements over the festive season!"

He said this with such force that poor Mole felt he had committed a crime even to suggest such an idea.

"Mole," continued Toad very seriously, "I could not possibly see anyone over Christmas. For one thing, I shall have relatives staying and they, or rather she, would not approve. Added to which, there is the plain fact that for me this is not and can never again be a time to celebrate, as I would have thought you might have known. No, no! It is quite impossible! Indeed, I feel most upset that you should spoil our tea by suggesting such a thing!"

With this, Toad took out his red spotted handkerchief

and dabbed at his eyes with an apparently genuine show of misery and grief.

"But, Toad..." began the bewildered Mole, "I simply – I mean to say – O *dear*!"

For Toad had risen from his chair now and before the Mole could ask more – or enquire who "she" might be – he had escorted Mole to his front door, bringing the tea to a summary end.

In the days following, try as he might, the Mole had been unable to rid himself of the dark mood that then overtook him. For Toad's inexplicable attitude had stirred within the Mole's heart memories he preferred to leave buried. He had reminded Mole of his great regret that over the years he had lost touch with his family. He had not heard anything directly from his errant brother for at least a decade, and only had news via a third party that a son had been born, and that Mole therefore had a nephew.

As for his much-loved older sister, who had cared for him when he was young through those difficult years of his mother's illness and from whom he had learnt so much of the domestic arts, she had moved as far away from their place of birth in one direction as he had in another, and sadly communication had in recent years ceased altogether.

Though every Christmas the Mole took pains to send each of these lost siblings his loving greetings at their last-known address, he had heard nothing for so many years that he had been forced to admit he ought to give up trying. Yet old habits and hopes die hard, and they had left in the Mole a lingering and bittersweet desire to share once more a Christmas with others with that same joy as he had felt when he was younger.

Till now the Mole had never allowed the black dogs of despair that sometimes barked at his door at Christmastide to enter his home. Instead, he decorated Mole End yet more brightly, lit his candles more plentifully, and made and ate his seasonal savoury delicacies and sweetmeats with ever more relish. Then, when the darkness of the evening finally fell upon Twelfth Night, he would light a fire that was especially bright. This was

the night his father had taught him to wassail the orchard of his childhood home. These days he had no orchard, yet the Mole would make a draught of wassail all the same, for old times' sake. Then he would take it hot and steaming across the fields towards the River Bank to toast the crab-apple tree that grew there, from which, each year, he gathered enough apples to make cider and jelly for the winter months.

After this ritual, Mole would return to his home, and with the heady scents of his Twelfth Night Pie baking in his range, he would take down the decorations one by one and put them away for next year. Then he would cut himself a generous slice of pie and sit back in his most comfortable armchair, staring into the fire. Finally, when its embers began to die and midnight approached, he would stand and raise his glass – filled with his famous sloe and blackberry – and drink a toast to those he loved.

"To my parents," he would say, "whose memory will never die. And to my errant brother, that he may find greater happiness in the year now started than perhaps he had in the one just ended. Lastly, to my beloved sister, wherever she may be, that this coming year may see our reunion at last. A Happy Christmas to you all, my dears, and to all who love you!"

Such, for more years than he cared to remember, had been the way of the Mole's festive season.

Perhaps Toad's tea-time rejection might not have mattered had it not been prefaced by a curious lack of enthusiasm for the coming Christmas season from

Mole's other River Bank friends, namely Ratty, Badger and Otter.

The truth was that this year of all years the Mole had very good reason for believing that in the festive department things might improve at last, and improve greatly! In the past eighteen months his happy acquaintance with the practical Water Rat, the wise Badger, the stout-hearted Otter and the exalted and munificent Toad had, as he had thought, blossomed into friendship.

It was a friendship forged in all the excitements and adventures that had followed Toad's imprisonment for stealing a motor-car and his subsequent escape from gaol. Most notable, perhaps, was the battle with the weasels and stoats from the Wild Wood after they had so impudently taken possession of Toad Hall – a memorable battle in which the Mole had excelled himself and earned his friends' respect and admiration.

Through the long, contented summer months – more blissful than any he had known since his childhood – hardly a day had gone by that had not found him at the River Bank, there to greet the Rat and pass the time of day. Or, better still, to share a luncheon-basket filled with the good food and drink the domesticated Mole took such pride in providing and which added so much to a day's boating and conversation.

In this way the River Bank and its inhabitants had introduced him to a whole new way of life. It had never occurred to the Mole in his earlier years that there might come a time in his life when he would be permitted to mix in such distinguished and exciting company, and be counted among their friends. They had made him realise that he must not be quite so reclusive, and that it might be better to enjoy the present rather than dwell on a past that could never come back, not even for a day or two, however much he might wish it.

So when autumn came, the Mole had begun to harbour secret hopes for a more sociable festive season. Indeed, modest though he was, the Mole might have justifiably expected to see his considerable contribution to River Bank society recognised and celebrated in some small way at Christmastide. Which was why Mr Toad's peremptory rejection of his seasonal invitation had hit him so hard.

Yet he had to admit that there had been other intimations that Christmas was not celebrated quite as he would have liked along the River Bank. He had, for example, sent out early feelers concerning their plans to each of his new friends, but not one of them had responded positively about the idea of sharing an evening or two at his home over Christmas. The Mole had been so perturbed by this that he had consulted the Otter upon the subject.

As gently as he could the Otter had tried to make the Mole understand that the practical Rat had little interest in something as frivolous as mere festivity, especially at a time when winter storms caused trees to fall and the River to rise, which made it a busy and dangerous season for one whose task in life was to see that the River Bank stayed safe and manageable for those who lived along it.

"You might see him along the Bank somewhere," explained the Otter, "and you might even get a wave from him, but that's all. Don't make the mistake of thinking he's idling, for he's hard at work communing with the River. She can rise to her limits in minutes, and if there's nobody about to open the sluices into the canal – and Ratty's the only one who knows exactly how and when to do that – then we'd all be flooded, at goodness knows what cost to life, and limb, and property! Why do you think there've been no serious floods since Ratty took control of such matters?"

"O my!" the Mole had said abashed. "I had no idea. I shan't disturb him over Christmas at all then!"

"Best not, old fellow," said the Otter.

"But surely Badger does not have such grave responsibilities, so perhaps you could explain why *he* was reluctant to commit himself to visiting Mole End?" said the Mole. "I made clear that any time would do –"

Otter laughed and said, "Badger always goes into retreat when the darker weather comes and rarely puts his nose outside his own front door, let alone inside anyone else's! He prefers to lose himself in his books and studies till the winter's passed."

"O!" said the Mole, disappointed once again.

"But surely *you* might like to come over to Mole End, Otter?" suggested the Mole quietly.

Otter shook his head.

"I'll give it a miss, Moly, old chap, if you don't mind. I – well, I have work to do," said he vaguely, "and I'm not much good at that sort of thing."

"O my!" said the Mole very quietly indeed. But he was not ready to give up yet. "But what about Toad? Surely *Toad* has no good reason to be unsociable at this time of year, has he? So *he* might like –?"

"You could always ask him, I suppose," said the Otter noncommittally, "but – well – he usually has relatives staying up at the Hall and they keep him busy for most of the time."

"O! I see," said the disappointed Mole. "Well then!"

It was against this disheartening background that the Mole had had his tea with Toad, and it explained the black mood he fell into in the weeks thereafter.

To think that none of his companions wanted to see him in the days ahead, not one of them! They who had become such good friends in the summer months!

Now, with only three days to go, he sat listlessly poking at his parlour fire and toying with the cherished baubles and hangings, candleholders and ribbons in the two boxes of Christmas decorations he had brought down from his attic some days before. Till now, he had lacked the will to put them up. Suddenly, his hand happened upon a tin star, its gilt worn with time, its points blunted by use. It had been given to him by his sister, and no Christmas was the same without it.

"Happy Christmas, dear brother!" she had said so long ago. "Now and for ever!"

Mole's eyes filled with tears of fond memory and regret. He held the star to his chest and before long was weeping openly, expressing his utter wretchedness that, once more, he had to spend Christmas alone with nobody to share his simple celebrations.

Yet the Mole was not one to give in to self-pity for long, or to give up on his dreams. When yet another tear plopped on to the star in his hand it seemed he suddenly saw its light anew. He blinked back the tears, and a new look of determination came to his eyes. He stood up and fetched some more kindling for the fire to make sure it was burning as brightly as possible.

"I will *not*," he declared, putting the star in the centre of his mantel, "allow others to spoil my Christmas like this! Really, I will not!"

Then in a sudden frenzy he put up all his decorations, down to the last broken bauble and torn and tattered angel, accompanying this activity by cries and expostulations such as, "No! I will not have it! I *shall* enjoy myself! Christmas is for laughter not for tears! This Mole is not for turning!"

Why, in all his days he had never come across a community that offered such sociable fun during the rest of the year, but suffered from such a malaise during the festive season. It could not possibly be something *he* had said or done! No, surely there must be some secret about the River Bank and Christmas he did not know.

"It is most strange!" he told himself a thousandth time as he prepared to retire for the night. "I should feel so much happier if I understood what lies at the root of it all. If I can discover that soon then it might not be too late to do something before Christmas Eve. I shall begin tomorrow by going to the Village Post Office to collect my parcel. I can't put it off any longer."

The parcel contained gifts for his three friends that had been ordered back in October when he still naively thought he would be celebrating Christmas with them. He had received notification some days ago that it was ready for collection.

"Yes! It will do me good to get out. I shall set off first thing in the morning. What is more," he told himself when he was finally in bed, "I shall take the opportunity to call upon Otter again. No doubt he will tell me that I shouldn't bother with presents at all, but that will give me the opportunity of finding out what I need to know if I am to make an assault upon the River Bank's collective gloom. I shall go and consult him on this matter on my return from the Village tomorrow afternoon!"

Feeling much more cheerful and determined, the Mole blew out his candle and settled his head on his comfortable, familiar pillow.

* * *

Dawn brought a worsening in the weather, with storms in the offing, but the revitalised Mole cheerfully readied himself for his journey. Seeing that the fields by the River looked very muddy and close to flooding, he took the drier route, which brought him out on the road a little above the grand entrance to Toad Hall.

As he climbed over the stile and stood contemplating his journey west to the Village, he heard the sound of a horse and cart behind him. The approaching vehicle was clean and freshly painted green, with yellow lettering. It was one of those sturdy, well-made carts the better class of victualler use to supply and deliver their produce to the better class of customer.

On its side the Mole read the bold words "W. Baltry, Sole Proprietor, Lathbury and District: Game, Poultry and Quality Smoked Meats". The driver was a bewhiskered gentleman of late middle age and from the cut of his attire and his air of confidence, the Mole guessed that he might be Mr Baltry himself.

"Good morning, sir. My name is Mr Mole of Mole End and I am most happy to offer you festive best wishes," said the Mole cheerfully. "Are you by any chance on your way to the Village?"

"Indeed I am. Yer can take a ride with me if yer've a mind to't, with the compliments of the season!" he said, making room for the Mole on the seat beside him. "Baltry's the name and poultry's the game."

Mr Baltry was transporting Christmas fare: one large plucked goose, a splendid haunch of venison and a side of pork. In addition, there were two cages of scraggy chickens, three dead rabbits and some appetising pies.

"I've to call in at t' Hall first, though, to drop off the goose and venison. And I've a feeling that Mrs Ffleshe will take a fancy to the pork."

"Mrs Flesh?" repeated the Mole, momentarily puzzled.

"Beggin' yer pardon, sir, but it's pronounced 'Ffleshe' with two 'f's' and not 'Flesh' as in meat – she's inclined to be very particular on that point – as she is on just about everything else!"

He added this last in a low voice, rolling his eyes skywards.

"No doubt Mrs Ffleshe is the temporary housekeeper?" said the Mole, thinking it quite likely that Toad's regular housekeeper might have taken a holiday, which necessitated his employing a substitute to help entertain the relatives to whom the Otter had referred.

"'Er an 'ousekeeper?" cried Mr Baltry, turning the cart into Toad's gravelled drive. "Why she'd 'ave yer guts fer garters if she caught you sayin' that. I don't know exactly 'oo she is in relative terms, but I do know she might as well be 'is mother-in-law, fer the way she carries on."

"I don't believe he would ever get married," declared the Mole jocularly.

"I don't believe 'e would!" said Mr Baltry, laughing heartily. "'Specially not if it brings the likes of 'er to 'earth and 'ome."

"How did it happen, then?" enquired the Mole.

Mr Baltry was only too eager to tell him.

"When Mr Toad Senior died," he explained, "which he did, just like that, a dozen or more Christmases back, his brother, that's the present Mr Toad's uncle, what is known as Groat, 'oo made 'is millions in tea plantations in Ceylon and now lives in retirement near Manchester, sent 'is old nanny along to keep Mr Toad company at Christmas, or that was the reason 'e gave. The talk in t' Village was that Nanny Fowle, which was 'er name, 'ad spoiled 'is Christmases for a good few years and 'is wife said it's 'er or me. So Groat palmed 'er off on Toad, along with 'er daughter, who is the widow Mrs Ffleshe.

"Now, Nanny Fowle passed on a few years back but Mr Toad, 'oo's got a soft heart, couldn't say no to Mrs Ffleshe coming every year, and it's been the ruination of his Christmas, and 'alf the Village's too."

Just as the Mole was about to ask Mr Baltry to elaborate, for it seemed possible that here was a clue to the mystery of the gloomy River Bank Christmas, a sudden change came over Mr Baltry's cheerful face and he said in a low voice, "'Ere she comes now, so watch it!"

They had been making for the tradesman's entrance, but now the front door of Toad Hall opened and a woman emerged and stood staring at them from the top step.

"Is that you, Baltry?" she said in a voice of such sharply disagreeable command that it sent a weary rook that was resting on a nearby wall flapping for cover.

"It is, ma'am," said Baltry respectfully.

She was of solid, stocky build and though not quite large, nor yet quite broad, she was by any measure formidable. As she came down the steps and crunched across the gravel towards them she gave the impression of an army of Prussian soldiers engaged in an assault on an enemy position. When she arrived alongside she towered over Mr Baltry and also over his horse, which snorted feebly and dropped its ears in submission.

"Let me have a proper look at that goose," said Mrs Ffleshe, leaning into the cart.

She fingered the legs and breast of the bird assertively, leaving numerous dents in it. Then she turned her attention to the venison, bending down and sniffing at it, as a vulture might examine carrion.

"Passable," she said, "just."

Then her eyes fell on the side of pork.

"What's this?"

Mr Baltry sighed and said, "That's spoken for by His Lordship the Bishop's wife."

"Nonsense. I must have it," said Mrs Ffleshe at once, "for we have an extra guest at Christmas luncheon."

"I promised to deliver it to her this afternoon," said Baltry a mite feebly.

"Well, it's mine now," said Mrs Ffleshe, attempting to heave it out of the cart.

"Really, Mrs Ffleshe, if I was the King of Siam –"

"You're not and not likely to be," said she.

Then she pointed at the Mole and said, "Get your apprentice here to take it into the kitchen at once."

Before Mr Baltry could say anything the Mole was heaving the side of pork on to his own shoulder.

"Glad to oblige you, Mrs Flesh," said the Mole in a mischievously obsequious way.

"Its 'Ffleshe', with an 'e'," said Mrs Ffleshe; "and that'll be a tuppence a pound off your price, Baltry, for your lad's insolence."

* * *

The sight of Mole puffing in to the kitchen and laying the pork on the table came as quite a shock to Miss Bugle, the housekeeper.

"I am so sorry, Mr Mole, sir," she whispered. "Mrs Ffleshe takes up residence at the Hall for the Christmas period, you see, and she does have her particular way of running things. I'm sure that Mr Toad would apologise if only he knew."

The Mole laughed, for he rather enjoyed being taken for an apprentice. In fact, he was beginning to think he had been mistaken in his judgement of the River Bank at Christmas and that there was fun and jollity to be found hereabout after all.

He wished Miss Bugle the compliments of the season and though he did not know her well he took the liberty – for she looked rather in need of cheering up and he could well imagine why – of suggesting that he might drop her off some of his chestnut and prune compote on Christmas Eve.

To his surprise and dismay he saw tears come to Miss Bugle's eyes.

"O Mr Mole!" she said. "How kind of you to think of such a thing, for I'm sure no one else in the Hall will dare to, this side of Twelfth Night!"

This was a strange comment, and the Mole would have liked to pursue it, but Mr Baltry's negotiations were over and he was in a hurry to get on his way, so he said a hasty farewell to Miss Bugle and resumed his ride.

He found Mr Baltry in very good humour, for he had made a successful sale of the pork to Mrs Ffleshe.

"I thought you said that it was promised to someone else," said the Mole.

"Saying isn't always meaning," said Mr Baltry with a wink. "The likes of Mrs Ffleshe always like to feel they've got something someone 'igher in the pecking order wants, and they'll pay more for it, *and* be 'appier too, so where's the 'arm in telling her it's for the Bishop's wife? But now we must press on. I need to get to the Village and then back to Lathbury before dark."

The Mole judged it best to let him get on with the driving without further talk, for the wind was strong enough to toss the horse's mane and tail about, and rock the cart as well. Worse, it was driving spits of rain into their eyes. Only when they had crossed the bridge and headed west for a few miles did Mr Baltry speak again.

"I tell you," he said, shaking his head, "you wouldn't get me living in these parts, and never in the Village!"

"Why ever not?" asked the curious Mole.

"Folk down 'ere ain't got two halfpennies to rub together, times is so hard. The livestock's all gone, what with the sheep rot last year and the cow gangrene this. And the crops is no better!"

"No!" exclaimed the Mole, who was sorry to hear that the sheep had been ill and the cows poorly.

"Aye, and they say that the wheat round the Village has got the drone fly good and proper now, and there's no disputin' their taters are harbouring riddle worm. And, o' course..."

"Yes?" said the Mole, much alarmed by what he was hearing.

The poultryman dropped his voice to a confidential whisper, "... their sugar beet's taken the fluke root, and that's bad, very bad. Eat one of them, yer'll have the pustules by dawn. It's no wonder folks is deserting the Village like fleas off a dead dog fox."

"O dear, O dear. I had no idea," said the kind-hearted Mole. "In that case, may I ask what business is taking you to the Village yourself today?"

The poulterer laughed.

"Business? *There?*" Then, looking back at the produce he was carrying and understanding the reason for the Mole's query, he added, "Ah, it's not what you'd call business exactly. You see, the verger's wife's my sister, and seeing as 'er 'usband's not the man 'e was since 'is geese got the gander fly, I'm giving 'em some provisions for Christmas, and I've thrown in something for their neighbours too, seeing as they're close to starving. Mind you, that shouldn't be *my* job! But the local gentry's not what it was in the way of helping people out."

"Really?" said the Mole, realising that he must be referring to Toad of Toad Hall.

"My sister says that in the days of good old Toad Senior he was so quick to help and generous with doctor fees that there's no way you'd have red mite running riot among the hens like they have now."

"Not them as well!" gasped the Mole.

"Them and the rest!" came the reply. "Why it's common knowledge that every last pig in the Village has gone deaf, and some say the bees is twaddled as well, which don't give much hope for pollination of the kale come summer and we all know what *that* means!"

"What does it mean?" asked the Mole.

"Means the fish won't bite and the black fly'll swarm in consequence and bring back the plague and every man jack of 'em'll be pushing up daisies by next Christmas. If you ask me it's all up with the Village and the best thing now is for it to be eradicated and razed, and those poor devils remaining given free passage to Australia."

"You mentioned Mr Toad Senior," said the Mole to bring the conversation back to his present concerns.

"Only met him once," said Mr Baltry, "when the sister I mentioned took 'er son up to the Hall to be blessed. It was widely thought that the Village had stayed free of disease all those years because of Mr Toad Senior's special powers, so my sister said that he ought to lay hands on her Chesney, who was the youngest and the runt of the pack and 'ad rickets and all sorts. Toad Senior blessed him and 'e was cured and never needed braces and blinkers again."

"A miracle!" said the Mole.

"That's what we said. My sister wrote to the Pope in Rome to 'ave Mr Toad made a Saint but seein' as he was not a Catholic 'e wasn't, which is wrong in my opinion because religion shouldn't be allowed to get in the way of saintliness. You are or you aren't, I reckons."

"So Mr Toad Senior was popular?"

"That 'e was, just like his son after 'im, the present Mr Toad. But o' course things have changed since Mrs Ffleshe turned up for Christmas. You wouldn't think a small thing like that would have such a terrible effect."

"It has? And on the festive season locally?"

Though this was intended as a question, Baltry took it as a statement.

"You're right there, sir. To all intents and purposes for the twelve days of Christmas Mr Toad isn't the toad 'e normally is. As I said afore and I say again, she is as good a mother-in-law as a bachelor like 'im is ever likely to find, and since every married man knows what a disaster they can be, especially at Christmas, it's no surprise the effect she's 'ad. Which reminds me, don't eat no beans from the Village, they're all sluggified and not good for your – whoa, there!"

Mole had been so absorbed by the conversation that they had arrived at the crossroads at the heart of the Village without his realising it.

"Where shall I set you down?"

Mole could see the church to one side and the Public House to the other, with the Post Office not far off.

"This will do nicely," said he. "But before you go could you just explain –?"

"Can't stop, I'm afraid, for the mushrooms 'ereabout have contracted flux and that's catching when the wind blows hard from the north like it is today. If there weren't the moisture in the air keeping it down we'd all be dead by sunset. So if it's all the same to you, and wishing you the compliments of the season, and a Happy New Year, if you get that far, I'd prefer not to linger a second longer!"

· II ·
The Village

It was some time since the Mole had visited the Village, and then only briefly, but he remembered it as a busy, cheerful, thriving place. He was therefore surprised to find, considering it was a weekday morning, that the only sign of life was at the Public House across the way.

Its windows were lit by the flickering lights of candle and fire, and its paint was peeling, but its half-open door offered some kind of welcome to strangers. Mole therefore decided that once he had collected his package he would pay it a visit and see what he could find out from the locals about Mrs Ffleshe and her effect on the community.

On his way to the Post Office, he passed the church and noticed at once that it lacked any sign of festive decorations, within or without. Upon its porch door, whose ironwork was rusty and whose frame showed signs of woodworm, the following dismal notice had been pinned:

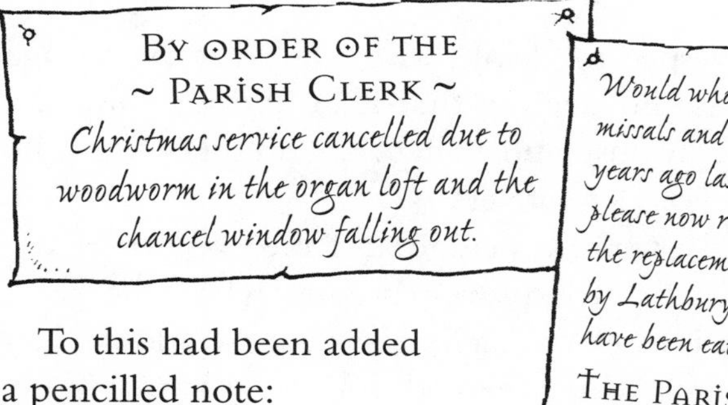
BY ORDER OF THE
~ PARISH CLERK ~
Christmas service cancelled due to woodworm in the organ loft and the chancel window falling out.

To this had been added a pencilled note:

Would whoever removed the missals and hymn books four years ago last Michaelmas please now return them as the replacements lent to us by Lathbury St Nicholas have been eaten by rats.
†THE PARISH CLERK

Pondering these unhappy announcements, the Mole carried on to the Post Office, where he was alarmed to read another notice:

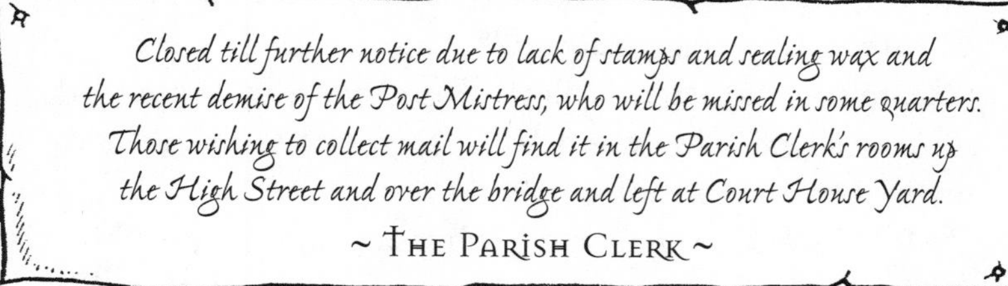
Closed till further notice due to lack of stamps and sealing wax and the recent demise of the Post Mistress, who will be missed in some quarters. Those wishing to collect mail will find it in the Parish Clerk's rooms up the High Street and over the bridge and left at Court House Yard.
~ †THE PARISH CLERK ~

Feeling increasingly anxious that he would never see his parcel, the Mole proceeded towards the bridge, which he could see a little way ahead. On his way, he passed what had been a thriving Village shop when he was last here, but which was now boarded up.

Closed permanently due to decline in seasonal business and the deathwatch beetle causing collapse of shelves and counter and loss of till into the basement. The Parish Clerk has the beetle powder. He's normally in but may not be. Try him at Court House Yard.

~ THE PARISH CLERK ~

"O my!" gasped the Mole, for he felt that the Village was in such rapid decline that if he did not find the Parish Clerk's house and collect his presents soon, he might never get them at all.

He walked over the bridge and into a part of the Village he had not explored before, where he soon found Court House Yard, a lonely square overlooked by a grand building which seemed to be the Court House.

There was a noticeboard declaring "Parish Clerk's Residence", upon which there were a number of announcements in the now familiar writing.

The most prominent read, *"Duty calls! He who is normally in is out. Back at 11 o'clock. Closing soon after for Christmas Day, if work allows."*

"'Signed the Parish Clerk'," intoned the Mole with some respect. This was a Village official who certainly seemed to take his job seriously.

Mole looked to right and left but saw no one resembling a parish clerk, nor anyone else for that matter. His pocket watch showed him he had only quarter of an hour to wait, but as it was cold he decided to keep himself busy by examining what he had always thought, till he had seen the imposing Court House, to be the Village's main architectural feature, namely the bridge.

A woman emerged and stood staring at them from the top step... *(p. 20)*

Its size and splendour spoke of more prosperous days in the Village. A point affirmed by an inscription upon it which read, *"Erected by public subscription to the glory of the Monarch, 1766."*

Mole was just contemplating the rushing water beneath, and thinking that the moment his business was complete he might be wise to return to Mole End, when he espied another building he had never noticed before which projected downstream from the bridge and was part of its structure.

It was square and squat and quite small and had only one narrow window, as far as he could see, which was barred and set curiously high from the ground. He retraced his steps and saw that there was an old gate, its padlock and chain rusted and broken, which opened upon some steep steps that went down the side of the building and stopped at a low arched door, which had some substantial ironmongery in the way of chains and padlocks, and a little square grille.

"Odd," he said to himself, "and strange."

Mole, who was always curious about such things, succeeded in pushing open the gate and venturing down. There was evidence of past flooding on the lower steps in the form of waterborne debris – reeds, bits of wood, rope and the remnants of a swan's nest.

Standing on tiptoe, he was able to look through the grille. In the dim light cast by the window he could make out a flat stone bench into which were set iron rings, with thick chains hanging from the wall above it. In one corner there was an ancient wooden chair of very sturdy construction, and near it, upon the floor, an earthenware bowl of the kind used by criminals for their ablutions. In another corner the Mole could see a culvert or well of some kind, which he surmised must fall away into the river itself.

"Why, this is a gaol!" said the Mole to himself in astonishment.

This was immediately confirmed when the Mole noticed a battered old sign, its paint peeling and its lettering faded. After considerable effort, he was just able to make out the words, *"Village Pound – examine your conscience and your ways all ye who enter here, especially sneak-thieves, pickpockets, felons, traitors, poll collectors, vagrants, nags and witches, to whom every justice shall be shown but no mercy given."*

Underneath this a further inscription announced, *"Renewed by Act of Parliament 1781, this place of retribution and fitting punishment under the jurisdiction of the Lord of the Manor & Court Baron. Hereinafter, as decreed, are listed the trials and tortures to be administered upon the innocent till proved guilty, all in the interests of Justice and for the good of..."*

All else was indecipherable. The Mole shivered, for the place had about it an air of past punishment, and long servitude, and was made cold and damp by the proximity of the river. This he now saw flowed hard against the gaol's walls, and by the look of its colour and the weather it was about to rise even further.

Shivering again, and by now much concerned by the river's rise, the Mole hurried up the steps and back to the Parish Clerk's residence.

He was greatly relieved when the door was opened by a tall, gaunt man, dressed in an old-fashioned black frock coat, who in response to the Mole's query as to whether or not he was the Parish Clerk, responded thus: "By election and decree and the powers vested in me by the Lord of the Manor I have been, presently am, and shall till my dying day continue to be, unless deposed by statute or proven guilty of treason and or treachery to the Lord of Session, the Clerk of this ancient Parish."

"You are the gentleman who has signed various notices throughout the Village?" enquired the Mole politely.

The gentleman's pallid face suffused briefly with pleasure. "You have read, marked and learned them?"

"Some of them," said the Mole judiciously.

"Then please come into my office," said the Clerk.

Mole followed him, expecting to be shown into some small room where there might be a few papers, a ledger or two, and, perhaps, a Bible and some Acts of Parliament. But no, they went down a flagged and echoing corridor that opened into a great antechamber with huge wooden benches around its vast perimeter all lit by a skylight. At its far end were three varnished oak doors, the first of which carried the notice "Legal Gentlemen and Witnesses". The other two were labelled "The Judge" and "The Condemned".

"Go in there," instructed the Parish Clerk, pointing (to the Mole's considerable relief) to the first door, "while I don my robes."

Mole found himself in a room even vaster than the antechamber. Like the Village Gaol, it was lit by small, narrow, barred windows set high into the walls, through which a cold winter light filtered. Here and there a little extra illumination was provided by candles in brass holders, which showed it to contain some wooden seats in serried ranks like pews, a witness box, a jury box, a bench behind which were three huge judge's chairs decorated with heraldic devices, and various other nooks and crannies for court officials.

As his eyes grew used to the gloom the Mole observed at one end a curious set of ancient stone steps much worn by use. They rose towards a door above the general level of the room, which appeared to go straight outside. Above its lintel, in red and gold, were the words, *"Ye Who Have Been Found Guilty, Prepare to Meet Thy Doom!"*

The Parish Clerk appeared suddenly from another door and, to the Mole's amazement, took what appeared to be the Judge's seat.

Thumping a gavel upon the Bench and quite startling poor Mole, he said, "Take the witness box!"

The Mole did as he was told.

"Your reason for being here?"

"I have come to –"

"A moment – we must observe the proprieties. Are you willing to take the oath?"

"Er – which one?"

"To tell the truth and nothing but."

"I normally do," said the Mole.

"Good," said the Parish Clerk. "Then we can dispense with that. Let me repeat my question in simpler terms so that its meaning is plain to you. Why (which is to say what reason can you give) are (which is of the verb 'to be' and refers to your corporeal presence) you (which is to say that which is invested in your body namely your soul) here (which refers not only to place but circumstance, and in that, to the cause of your coming)?"

"To collect a parcel that was sent to the Post Office, where I read a notice that said –"

"I know what it said," said the Parish Clerk testily, "since I wrote it myself, from which a witness of normal intelligence might be expected to deduce that I have no need to be told what it said."

The Mole stayed silent.

"Well?" said the Parish Clerk.

"May I have it, please?" asked the Mole.

"Is this the item?" came the response.

Mole's interrogator produced a package from under the bench which even from the witness box the Mole could see was addressed to himself.

"Yes, it is."

"Can you show the court proof of your identity?" asked the Parish Clerk, keeping a firm hold on the package.

"I – I –" said the Mole, rather taken aback.

"This is addressed to Mr Mole of Mole End."

"Yes, that's me," said the Mole with some satisfaction.

"Can you at least demonstrate that you are that Mole, seeing as there may be others?"

"I have a pocket watch with my name inscribed upon it. It was given to me by my sister the last time I saw her, to mark the occasion when I moved south and took up residence at Mole End."

The Mole proffered his pocket watch but the Parish Clerk showed no great interest in it.

"It might be stolen and used as evidence against you in your trial as a sneak-thief," he said wearily, "and we do not want that today, because it is the beginning of my annual holiday. A more substantial trial, for arson, let us say, or capital treason, something I might get my teeth into, now that would indeed make my Christmas a jolly and festive one, for I am due for retirement and have never yet been privileged to act as Clerk at such an occasion. Mere sneak-thievery is not worth the candle (which is to say the festive candle). Ha! Ha!"

The Parish Clerk let out several more of these strange sounds before Mole realised that he was laughing at his own little joke and that it might be as well for him to join in, which he did, much to the Clerk's pleasure.

"You seem honest, you sound honest and, what is most convincing of all, you look like a mole. In that respect at least you are not an impostor, which is more than I can say for the last gentleman who stood there."

"And who was that?" enquired the Mole with some interest.

"It was a weasel masquerading as a stoat and attempting to fool us, but failing. I dealt with him severely."

The Parish Clerk glanced at those steep steps the Mole had noticed earlier.

"He was the first person in one hundred and seventy-eight years to be sent up those steps, though in the event he pleaded with me to let him off with a fine, which I did. I shall not be so weak again! I would not want you, Mr Mole of Mole End, to be so condemned, eh?"

"Er, no," said the Mole.

"Therefore, take your parcel and cause no breach of the peace during your sojourn in our Village and no harm will befall you, for in the absence of the Lord of the Manor you are under the surrogate protection of the Clerk to this ancient Parish, which is to say myself, the Parish Clerk."

"I am most grateful," said the Mole, vacating the witness box and approaching the bench, "and if I might be so bold –"

"Permission is hereby granted," said the Clerk.

"I am glad indeed to see that the ancient traditions of law, order and justice are still alive and well in our land."

Again the Parish Clerk's parchment face coloured with pleasure.

"Quite so, Mr Mole, quite so. And there is another tradition which it is my duty to follow. It has long been the custom for myself, as Parish Clerk, and my predecessors right back to Arild the Hornless, who was a Viking, to visit the Public House on the eve of Yule. As my last duty before Christmas has been completed, it would be my pleasure to invite you to be my guest and partake of the Village Chalice, whose depths are plumbed on this sole occasion each year."

Mole agreed at once, for he enjoyed history and tradition, and saw that once again one need only look in the right place to find the spirit of Christmas.

"I imagine you must know the history of this chamber, and this office, better than any man alive."

"It may be so," said the Clerk.

"You made mention of the Lord of the Manor," said Mole, as the Parish Clerk, still wearing his official robes, came round the side of the bench. "I was wondering who that might be, since I have never heard of such a position in relation to the Village. Is it perhaps an office that is now defunct, the bloodline of that office being long extinct?"

The Parish Clerk sighed heavily.

"He lives, Mr Mole, but no longer in the Parish. Mr Toad Senior was his predecessor and *he* took his duties seriously, often honouring us with his presence on the Bench. But Mr Groat..."

The Mole's ears pricked up. He had heard that name before, and only this very morning. Why, surely, that was Toad's uncle?

"... Mr Groat left the Parish rather under a cloud some decades ago and in consequence much, indeed most, which is to say virtually all, affairs of the Village have ground to a halt for lack of his imprimatur. I have done the best I can but it is not enough."

"This gentleman, Mr Groat, am I to understand he is the uncle of Mr Toad, of Toad Hall?"

"You are, though I'd rather you described him as the brother of Mr Toad Senior."

"Which is to say Toad's late father?" said the Mole.

"You know Mr Toad?" asked the Parish Clerk. "I believe you are too young to have known his father."

"Yes, I do know Toad," said the Mole. "I had tea with him at Toad Hall only a few days ago."

"You have actually *spoken* with him?" asked the Clerk in wonderment and with evident respect.

"He usually speaks to me, actually," said the Mole. "It tends to be rather difficult to get a word in edgeways when he is in the room."

"Then, sir, then –"

"Yes?" said the Mole, surprised at the animation that had suddenly come to the Parish Clerk's face.

"– you are in the position to do me, and the Village as well, a service, a very considerable service."

"Am I?" said the surprised Mole.

"You are. But let us first retire to the Village hostelry."

They set off across the bridge and then by way of the High Street to the Public House. With its guttering candles, struggling fire and dark shadows, it seemed rather unwelcoming at first.

The landlord was a man of gloomy expression who gruffly greeted the Parish Clerk with, "Yer've come fer yer annual quart, then?"

"I have," said the Parish Clerk, "which is to say –"

"Which is to say 'ere it be," said the landlord, thumping a great frothing tankard down upon the bar. "And what'll it be fer yer friend?"

"The same, please," said the Mole.

"Right you are. Nah then, wot abaht yer food?"

"What's on the menu?" asked the Parish Clerk.

"Christmas Fare, of course. There's matured turkey from last year, and some red cabbage wot turned back to green five months ago, and tatties mushed with onions."

"They're fresh, are they?" enquired the Mole.

"Fresh as the month they was mashed, which is February last," said the landlord. "And very flavoursome they are too. Proved particularly popular with the passing trade, for they've never come back to complain. And the beans is good –"

"Er, no beans for me, if you don't mind," said the Mole hastily, remembering the poulterer's warning. Nor did he like the sound of anything else he had been offered. "Perhaps I'll just have this fine tankard of beer."

"Suit yerself."

The Mole saw that there were a few more gentlemen of varying ages scattered about the parlour, all looking beaten down and miserable.

"Take a pew," said the Parish Clerk, indicating what he saw was indeed a pew, judging by its length and shape. "Now, where were we?"

So it was that the resourceful Mole found himself seated in the Village Public House, surrounded by a group of men who, though nearly as mournful as the landlord, proved willing enough to talk.

Of the conversation that ensued the Mole never spoke in detail, but it was enough to confirm that festive matters had reached even more parlous a state in the Village than they had along the River Bank.

Some blamed Mrs Ffleshe directly, while others, like the Parish Clerk, laid the blame at the door of the departed Groat and said dereliction of his duty was at the root of all their woes.

"How can a ship come to port rudderless?"

"How can mangels be lifted when the tines 'ave gone missin'?"

"Yer can't 'spect the cows to come 'ome with no cowherd to bring 'em!"

Mole saw where the problem lay, but could well understand why it might be that since Mrs Ffleshe's coming the once-festive and sociable Toad had not been in the mood to grace their company.

"He be barred from coming 'ere," explained the coughing man by the fire, a rodent catcher who made the Mole feel decidedly uneasy. "It's because that woman says 'e spends too much, which is a rum go, seein' as 'e's related to the Lord and Lords is meant to spend, otherwise what's the point?"

"The Lord?" queried the Mole, though by now he was getting the gist of things.

"Of the Manor."

"And of Session, or be you wanting to forget that, eh Daniel?" responded another. The others laughed.

"Daniel here is the last living man to have been arrested and arraigned, imprisoned and tried by the Lord of Session of the Village, which is to say the Court Baron."

"I was clapped in irons by *his* great-grandfather," said Daniel in an aggrieved voice, pointing to the Parish Clerk, "and only pardoned because news of Boney's defeat was proclaimed that same day. But not before –"

"You tell the gentleman," said the others, who seemed to gain pleasure from hearing an old tale repeated.

"– aye, not before I was put to the rack and stretched a yard at least and then spitted on the fire and so roasted my eyebrows never grew back, and then squashed under a millstone till I was a goner."

"Tell 'im what brought you back to the land of the livin'," one of his companions called out.

"Blessed Toad Senior it was, he who was nearly sainted for his good works; he who kept the Village free of the riddles when all others in the land 'ad it; he who's been on that very pew where you're sat and turned water into porter with a wave o' his blessed hand at this very table. Mr Toad Senior! He took one look at me in the coffin – for that's 'ow far it got – and said 'I am the Lord! Rise up, Daniel, and walk to the pub!' and I 'eard 'is voice and though I was comfortable where I was I couldn't say no. It's as true as I'm sitting 'ere now, and seein' as yer buying I'll have a treble porter with a dash of mild."

The Mole stayed in the company of these agreeable gentlemen a good deal longer than he should, and it was a testimony to his friendly good spirits that the mood in the hostelry became a good deal more festive than it had been. He learnt much, but most of all that they regretted the passing of the old days when the Lord of the Manor took his duties seriously, and made sure that those in the Village who served the Hall through the year, and very many more who did not or were not able, were looked after with free food and drink, and fuel as well, through the harsh winter months.

"It's no good hopin' we'll ever 'ear from that Groat," the Mole afterwards remembered them saying – but who said it he could not quite recall, for his memory of the details was fuzzy – "and as long as he do stay away we'm doomed to be whittled and stoomed till the only thing left o' us is the stitching of our boots!"

Nor was the Mole able to remember quite what it was that the Parish Clerk asked him to do as a favour to them all, for by then the Clerk's voice was unsteady, as he was unused to anything stronger than well water.

When all but he seemed fast asleep and quite unwakeable, the Mole's fuddled attention was drawn by the sound of rain against the window. He saw that the afternoon was advancing rapidly towards dusk and so, making his excuses to the sleeping throng, he picked up his package and stepped outside.

Before he set off on the long journey home, his curiosity drew him back to the bridge, where he paused again to look down at the gloomy gaol below. Then he went on to Court House Yard and shook his head in astonishment at the memory of what lay within and at the stories that the Parish Clerk had told him.

Finally, he walked round to the rear of the building, searching for the dreadful door he had noticed earlier from inside.

And there it was! A heavy, nailed and arched portal set high in the wall with no sign of any way down except vertically, straight into the now-raging waters of the river beneath.

"O my!" whispered the Mole to himself, suddenly glad that the days of ancient justice were over and more humane methods of trials and punishment now in vogue.

With this more cheerful thought upon him, the Mole walked back along the High Street and headed for home by way of the muddy road he had come up earlier that day with the poulterer. He reflected to himself that the visit had greatly cheered him, and the friends he had made and the ideas they had unwittingly given him left him much to think about.

He stopped only once along the way, for as his head

cleared with the fresh air so his memory came back, and he remembered the favour that the Parish Clerk had asked, and his rash undertaking to try to fulfil it.

"Yet I wonder if I might!" he exclaimed more than once. *"I wonder if I dare?"*

· III ·
Taken Alive

Darkness had descended when Mole finally reached the crossroads near Canal Bridge and familiar territory once more. He was now quite close to Otter's house, and he had not forgotten his intention of calling on him on his way home. In any case, he felt a little tired and in need of some refreshment before the final haul across the bridge and over the fields to Mole End.

"O, it's *you*, Moly!" cried the Otter when he opened his door to Mole's knock. "Whatever brings you out on such a rough night?"

Mole was very pleased to find the Otter at home, for

his path had taken him perilously close to the Wild Wood. The Mole was never a cowardly animal – just the opposite – but he was always a prudent one, and the various hisses, squeals, roars and wailings that emanated from the depth of the Wood boded ill, so he had hurried along the path as quickly as he could. When he saw that there was no light in Otter's house he had naturally grown doubly fearful at the prospect of a lonely return along the same route. So when his knock was answered so soon and so cheerfully by the Otter, Mole was greatly relieved.

"But why are you sitting in the dark, Otter?" asked the Mole.

"Ah! Yes!" said the Otter as he pressed a warming drink into his friend's hands. "I fear your unexpected coming may have disturbed a little ruse Ratty and I are just now involved in to catch out the weasels."

"A ruse?" wondered the Mole, who knew little of such things.

"We have reason to believe that the weasels or the stoats, or possibly both acting together, have been causing damage to the equipment Ratty and I keep along the River Bank for our mutual use – nets, poles, marker buoys and pruning gear. For several nights Portly and I have made a show of staying at Ratty's, then, each night, under cover of darkness, I have come back here in secret to keep a watch on things. It is as well your knock was clear and distinct, otherwise –"

Otter produced a fierce-looking boathook, which he had clearly intended to apply to the head and posterior of any weasel or stoat that came by up to no good.

"O my!" said the startled Mole, rubbing his head as if he himself had been struck by the Otter.

"We can't let 'em get away with it, Mole. What with flooding and ice, the River is a dangerous place in the winter, and only Ratty and I have the knowledge to make things safe."

"Quite so," said the Mole, very much impressed by the Otter's determination and courage on others' behalf. "I am sorry if I frightened them off before you could put your theory to the test."

"It couldn't be helped, Moly. But did you hear anything, or better still, *see* anything?"

"I heard many strange sounds from the direction of the Wild Wood," said the Mole with some feeling, "but nothing else, or nearly nothing."

"*Nearly* nothing?" asked the Otter.

"Well, when I was at the crossroads and was about to turn down to visit you here I am almost certain I heard the sound of running feet from the direction of the Iron Bridge."

"Running feet, eh!" cried the Otter, rising. "Near the Iron Bridge! You should have told me this before. Here, put your coat back on at once, I may need reinforcements. Hurry, Mole, hurry – and you had better carry this as protection!"

Mole was alarmed to have a fierce-looking cudgel placed in his hands. Not for the first time since he had made the acquaintance of the River Bankers, the quiet and unassuming Mole found himself thrust into a risky venture of a kind he would normally have done his very best to avoid.

Who was he to go off in the night in pursuit of weasels and stoats, cudgel in hand? And anyway, had he not made a point of visiting Otter's house for a very different purpose indeed?

"Er, Otter?" he essayed. "I did not really call upon you tonight to take up arms against the weasels and stoats. In fact, I was rather hoping you might give me some advice. You see –"

"Advice?" cried the distracted Otter as he locked his front door. "Advice about what?"

"Well, about Christmas, actually," said the Mole, somewhat feebly.

"Christmas?" said the Otter, stopping for a moment in his tracks. "*Christmas?*"

Yes, you see, Otter," began the Mole, "I was just trying –"

"My dear Mole," said the Otter very firmly, "this is not the time to talk of Christmas. There are many in these parts who may not have a Christmas at all if the weasels and stoats are allowed to continue vandalising the River Bank. Have you any idea of the power of the River when she grows angry with floodwater?"

"I – I – I did not think," said the Mole, quite at a loss for words.

"No, you did not!" said the Otter. "Now, there's a

good fellow, and come along to give me some support against these thugs and hooligans."

"Thugs?" said the bewildered Mole in a timid voice. "Hooligans?"

"And murderers," growled the Otter, leading the way along the River Bank path.

"Murderers?" repeated the Mole unhappily, as he tagged along behind the Otter in the dark, all thoughts of his revitalised Christmas plans, which he had so wanted to talk about, quite gone from his mind.

Mole's silent misgivings were soon amply justified. The two animals crept through the tangled reeds of the River Bank till they had the Iron Bridge dimly in view up-river, with the canal off to their left. There, in the chill, damp darkness, the increasingly nervous Mole was left to lie low in the reeds while the Otter went on ahead to investigate.

Feeling alone and vulnerable, he was beginning to shiver with cold when he heard the unmistakable sound of the enemy approaching from the Wild Wood. By the sound of things, they were dragging something heavy along with them.

"Otter!" he whispered hoarsely in the direction of the River Bank. "*Otter!* They are coming! Please, Otter, hear me!"

He did not dare move for he had no doubt their numbers were great, and he knew the sleek weasels and lithe stoats were fleeter of foot than he. He also thought it likely that the more they had to give chase the greater would be their appetites.

He hoped that his urgent whispers would not be heard against the River's murmur in the night, but when he called out Otter's name once more, quite desperate now, the dragging sound stopped at once and he heard ominous mutterings, as of villains deciding what to do next.

He did not have to wait long to find out. With one accord the night creatures moved rapidly forward towards where Mole lay, by now frightened out of his wits. Only when he saw their shadows looming from the undergrowth did he decide to break cover, cudgel in hand, and bravely charge them.

He was not sure what he hoped to achieve – perhaps to get a blow or two in first and then flee towards the bridge – but no sooner had he risen from the ground than he heard one of them grunt, "There!" and before he could even strike a blow, or see the enemy clearly, a strange shifting shadow engulfed him. He felt the harsh, rough entanglements of what seemed to be a net falling all about him, catching first at his cudgel, then at his arms, then enwrapped about his face and head till with a terrible cry he fell back upon the ground.

Worse followed, for the shadows stood over him, and the Mole felt buffets on his head and kicks about his body as they overwhelmed him and bundled him up so tightly that he could scarcely move a limb. Despite his brave struggles and now-muffled protests, he felt himself hoisted up by many hands and carried off to a fate that was so awful to contemplate that he fainted right away, and knew no more.

So it was that when the Otter returned some minutes later he found no Mole, no Mole at all. By the dim light of the winter night he could just make out an area of broken and flattened vegetation, with the Mole's cudgel lying abandoned nearby – graphic evidence of what had happened.

"Mole!" exclaimed the distraught Otter. "Moly, where are you?"

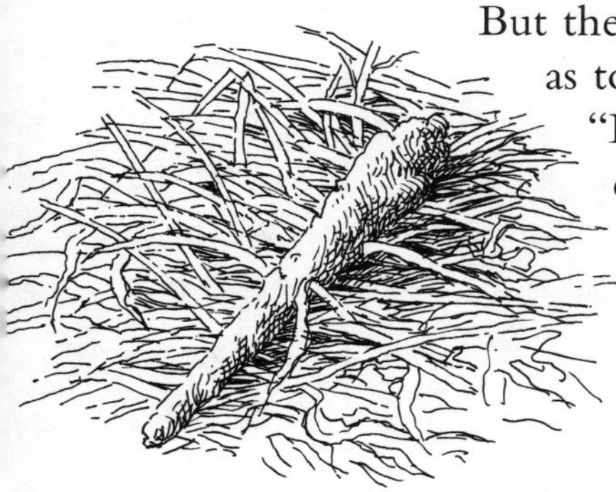

But the Otter was not so foolhardy as to hasten off in pursuit alone. "Badger's the only animal who can help Mole now!" he told himself, and without more ado he retraced his steps to the Bank and from there set off by safer and more familiar paths back into the Wild Wood towards Badger's home.

When Badger's door was opened – only after a long delay – the Otter was surprised to be confronted not just by the Badger, but also by the Water Rat as well, both heavily armed.

"My dear fellow," said the Badger, "you should have said it was you. Whatever are you doing here in the dead of night?"

"You must come quick, Badger, there's no time to lose. Mole's been taken by the weasels and stoats!"

"Mole?" repeated the Badger uncomprehendingly.

"Yes, *Mole*," said the Otter. "For who else would I risk a journey through the Wild Wood on such a night as this, except perhaps yourself or Rat?"

"Humph!" said the Badger disbelievingly. "It is surely not like Mole to take risks, least of all in these parts, and it might well be that you are mistaken and the sensible Mole is at home, tucked up in bed and fast asleep."

"He is certainly *not* at home!" spluttered the Otter, exasperated at Badger's seeming lack of concern. "I say again, Mole has been –"

"I know what you *said*, Otter," responded the Badger calmly, "and I can guess what you would like Ratty and me to do. I suppose you would like us to set forth into the Wild Wood and rescue him?"

"Yes, that's exactly –"

"Can't be done," said the Badger abruptly, "not in the thick of night, and especially not this night. We have already been out on an expedition and were half-expecting a counter-attack from the weasels and stoats. And we really shouldn't stand out here where we are vulnerable. Better to discuss this further in safety."

He shepherded the protesting Otter inside and swiftly bolted his door.

"Now, come and sit by the fire and try not to worry," he said. "I very much doubt that so important an animal as Mole, who is known to be Badger's friend, would be harmed by the weasels and stoats."

"I tell you –" cried the Otter.

"Tell us by all means, old fellow," said the Rat with some asperity, for he was getting cold in the hall, "but pray come and do so in Badger's comfortable parlour!"

The Otter soon found himself sitting by the fire, a glass of mulled wine in his hand, as he tried to explain poor Mole's startling disappearance.

Poor Mole indeed – not for him the comfort of a warming winter drink and the pleasures of conversation and companions. Instead, that unfortunate animal had suffered a good deal of hurt and indignity since he had been so unceremoniously abducted. Now he found himself in mortal danger.

When he had come round he found himself inside a rough hessian sack of some kind. From the warmth – the uncomfortable warmth – of the place, and the muffled murmur of voices, he realised he was in the foul den of the villains who had captured him. It did not take him long to appreciate the gravity of his situation. The stuffy atmosphere in his sack was growing more clammy by the second, and he was conscious of an unwelcome heat beginning to warm him even as he heard the unmistakable bubblings of a cooking pot nearby. Only by a great effort of will did he prevent his terror from overcoming him. It was almost as if the weasels and stoats were merely waiting for the pot to be hot enough before they tipped Mole into it and started stewing him for dinner later that night.

"O my goodness! Now, what weapons do I have upon my person?" he asked himself, feeling from pocket to pocket. He soon found that his arsenal consisted of one fountain pen, a silver fruit knife (the one with a shell handle that had been his mother's), a handkerchief and, *ow!*, a large safety pin!

This find was a cheering discovery, and he resolved to stab at anyone who came near. What might be achieved if he started with the pin, followed up with the pen nib and then finished them off with the knife?

But such brave thoughts lasted only a few moments till he heard movement nearby. Then the bubbling grew louder as the range was stoked, followed by laughter and the sound of lids being lifted and knives being sharpened. By now, inside the sack it was almost hot and steamy enough to render him parboiled, and even braised – and the Mole felt himself growing strangely light-headed and confused.

"O dear," he told himself. "This will never do: they're going to cook me without tucking some thyme and bayleaves into the sacking, and I am sure I would taste better if they covered me with a rasher or two of fatty bacon. O my, to be cooked is not good, to be sure, but to be cooked badly is a tragic way to end one's days!"

He swooned once more, and when he next emerged into consciousness he found himself crying out, "Make sure you put some cranberry and onion confit on the table, for I'll taste a good bit better with that!"

Then sanity returned and he told himself, "No, I will not be put into the cooking pot meekly, if only to show that we of the River Bank are not so easily vanquished! I'm sure it's what Badger would advise and what Ratty would do!" And with that he lay still, safety pin in hand, ready to attack the moment the villains released him.

How very differently had Mole's friends passed the evening! How dolefully true is the adage that out of sight is very soon out of mind, especially when creature comforts are on offer!

No sooner had the Otter settled down by the fire to explain how it was that the Mole had been captured than he yielded to the heady comforts of food, drink and companionship.

"How much more I would enjoy these excellent crumpets," he was saying, "if only I knew for *certain* that poor Mole was still alive!"

A second glass of mulled wine and toasted crumpets as a rather unusual *hors d'oeuvre* to the mushroom stew that the Badger was cooking, plus the soothing effects of a warm fire, had calmed the Otter to such an extent that all urgency concerning Mole began to leave him.

"And yet," he mused, "there must be *some* way we can work out where he might be, so that we are ready to search for him at first light."

"The Wild Wood is a big place," said the Badger as he

stoked the fire under the stew to bring it to a final boil and helped himself to another crumpet, "and there are many holes and underground passages that would serve the role of dungeon for one such as Mole very well indeed. But –"

Just then there was a slight movement in the shadows to the left of the Badger's inglenook which stopped their conversation quite dead.

"Good heavens, Badger," cried the Rat. "In the excitement of Otter's arrival and disturbing intelligence we have quite forgotten those villainous thieves we captured earlier tonight."

"Thieves?" said the astonished Otter, raising himself from his semi-slumber.

"There, in that muddy sacking," explained the Rat, pointing to the wet bundle by the hearth. "Three stoats and a brace of weasel at least. Caught 'em thieving along the River Bank just near your house."

"Stoats?" cried the Otter angrily, rising to his feet and staring down at the sacking. *"Weasels?"*

"Yes," said the Badger, shaking his head. "They've always been the same, those animals. No standards, no values, no respect for property and people's liberty. One would have thought that the trouncing we gave them at Toad Hall earlier this year would have taught them a lesson, but not so! They get more and more impudent as the months go by. Still, I suppose we ought to release them now and take their names."

"We should," said the Rat, "and come to think of it they might give us some help in finding Mole."

"Help?" cried the roused Otter. "I should say they'll

give us some help – once I've given 'em the drubbing they deserve."

Without further ado he set about kicking at the sacking. "Villains! This is for our friend Mole, whom your colleagues have abducted, and this as well, and this too!"

"Really, Otter, I think perhaps –" essayed the Rat, trying to restrain his friend.

"Desist, Otter, desist at once," cried the Badger, his voice deep with alarm. A drubbing was one thing, but a common assault quite another.

"Well..." growled the Otter, his ire suddenly gone, and feeling rather ashamed at getting so carried away.

As the other two regarded the sacking with a mixture of concern and curiosity, the Otter bent down and untied the cords that bound its top together.

"Out you come, villains!" he said, rising up once

more, and hoping the stoats and weasels had no more than a bruise or two apiece.

But the sacking remained ominously still, the shapes of bodies inside it accentuated by the flickering flames of the nearby fire, and made all the more lurid by the rise of steam from the hessian.

"I say, fellows," said the Water Rat, "this may be more serious than we thought. You don't think they have suffocated in there, do you?"

At once the three animals knelt down to release the captives, pulling open the mouth of the sack still further.

"Out you come!" ordered the Badger.

"Out?" cried an enraged voice from within the wet and steamy sack. "*Out?* I'll come out, all right!"

Out he certainly came, the bruised, abused, battered and furious Mole, like a rabbit bolting from its hole. Up and at 'em, safety pin and all!

"Take that! And that! And *that*!" he yelled, stabbing, pricking, hitting and punching, lunging and digging and making as much use of his tiny arsenal of weapons as he could. A Viking frenzy was upon him, which was why he did not immediately see that it was his friends he was assaulting.

"Have me for supper if you must!" he cried wildly. "But I shall fight and struggle all the way into the pot!"

Their cries of alarm and pain did nothing to stop him, but rather spurred him on, till one by one they retreated – the Badger to his bedroom, the Rat to the kitchen and the Otter behind a chair. Only then did the Mole give pause to see with clearer eyes, and realise with growing astonishment that he was in the Badger's sitting room.

"Villains!" he shouted (for he naturally thought that the weasels and stoats had somehow gained access to the Badger's home, and most likely had already eaten him for lunch). "Come out and show yourselves!"

Then, most sheepishly, most apologetically, his three friends left their hiding places and stood before the Mole, the very picture of contrition.

"But – but – but –" was all the astonished Mole could say, looking first at one and then another, then at the sacking by the fireside and the cooking pot, and finally understanding all.

It was a long time before anybody dared speak.

Finally, the Otter took it upon himself to attempt to mollify the aggrieved Mole.

"Well, now," he haplessly began, "I mean to say –"

"Best say nothing, old fellow," said the still angry Mole softly, rubbing his many bruises. But then, with a twinkle in his eye, for he was never one to hold a grudge, and always the first to laugh at himself and put the best complexion on things, he said more gently, "Best say nothing at all." Then, relaxing a little more, he said, "Do I not smell the heady scent of mulled wine?"

"You shall have some at once, dear Mole," said Ratty, hurrying to serve him.

"And crumpets, too?"

"I'll toast and butter you some fresh ones right away," said the Otter.

"And comfortable chairs?"

"Have mine, old fellow," said the Badger without hesitation, though no animal in living memory had ever sat in his chair before.

"Why, that's most obliging," said the Mole, sitting down with aplomb. "Very obliging. Ratty, perhaps you would be kind enough to charge my glass once more. And, Otter, I think that one more crumpet would go down well before I try that mushroom stew. O, and Badger, another cushion would – that's right, just there, yes, aah – and while you're at it, Badger, be a good chap and put another log on the fire."

Then a look of happy contentment came to him, and slowly to the others as well, as they began to enjoy that special peace and companionship that comes with the resolution of misunderstanding between good friends.

A second glass of mulled wine and toasted crumpets... *(p. 57)*

· IV ·
A Tale of Bleak Midwinter

"It is a pity," observed the Mole a little later, now calmed and comforted by food and drink, "that Toad is not here. I'm sure he would have enjoyed this evening."

"It *is* a pity," murmured the Badger, puffing at his pipe, "but I am afraid that his family duties for the festive season have now begun and so we shall see nothing of him till after Twelfth Night. There it is."

But there it definitely was *not*, so far as the Mole was concerned. He was determined to get to the bottom of the River Bank's festive malaise and do something about it.

"You said, Badger, 'there it is', as if you accepted the

situation. Forgive me for being bold, but I do *not* accept it. Toad must have his reasons for not celebrating Christmas, but I doubt that they are good ones, or ones he cannot be persuaded to abandon. But, since none of you is friend enough to tell me exactly what ails Toad, there is not much I can do to help."

He sighed in an exaggerated way to emphasise the distress he felt at not being taken into their confidence. Though it was very unlike his normal modest way to cause a fuss, he felt it was the least they deserved after their harsh treatment of him earlier.

A very long silence followed. The others all understood that it was best to wait to let Badger say what he must in reply. Finally, sighing rather as Mole himself had done, he began to speak.

"My dear friend, you are right to feel aggrieved and I apologize if we have seemed over-secretive. Let me try to explain how the situation was and now is, though the story starts even before *my* time."

As the Rat stoked the fire, and the Otter served up more mushroom stew, there unfolded a story so astonishing that the Mole could only shake his head at the folly of it all, and sigh at how one person could destroy the pleasure of so many; and then sigh again that the many should have allowed it to happen…

In the days of Toad's father, generally known as Toad Senior, Toad Hall certainly *had* been the fountainhead of things social and celebratory along the River Bank, just as the Villagers had told the Mole earlier.

Toad's father was good-natured and benign, and

though it is perhaps true that he spoilt and overindulged his son – the Toad they knew and grew irritated at and yet very much loved – at least he never put on the airs and graces that the wealthy sometimes do, and he did his best to stop Toad doing so either.

As for Christmas at the Hall, it was the local high point of the year, and Toad Senior saw to it that those in the Village who regularly supplied the Hall with the goods and services that a great establishment needs were remembered and rewarded. So too were those individuals and families who needed support when the cold months of winter descended. In fact, there was not a family in the area who in one way or another did not find that their festive fire shone more brightly for the concern, generosity and seasonal thoughtfulness of the occupants of Toad Hall.

The trouble began a year after Toad Senior's sad demise, which took place at Christmas.

"Didn't Toad step into his shoes and continue the Hall's tradition?" inquired the Mole, for this aspect of the matter had not been touched on at all by Mr Baltry or the Parish Clerk.

"Of course he *wanted* to," said the Badger. "That animal may have many faults but none can deny his generosity of spirit and of pocket, and his willingness to help others, if only he can be persuaded to forget himself for a moment! Yes, I believe that he very much wanted to continue his father's festive tradition of generosity. But you see, Mole, he was utterly prevented from doing so!"

Up to this moment, Mole's expression had been

simply curious; now, as the truth emerged, it darkened, and his brow furrowed.

After some months of grief and mourning Toad recovered sufficiently to host the Village's Summer Fete. When autumn came and the nights lengthened, Toad joined in the Village's Guy Fawke's celebration in relatively high spirits, and all seemed set fair for Yuletide. None doubted that things would be much as they were before, though perhaps a little subdued that year out of respect for the memory of the late Toad Senior.

Then, in early December, a telegraphic communication arrived at Toad Hall for Toad. The source of the message was that smoke-blackened city in the north of the country to where Toad's Uncle Groat, his father's younger brother, had recently retired after a lifetime of fortune-making in the wide world.

"Of *that* wretched scion of the family, I shall say no more than this," growled the Badger, interrupting himself. "He is Toad Senior's younger brother and unfortunately he seems never to have recovered from the fact that, being the second-born, he is not heir to Toad Hall and its estates. As a consequence, he developed from an early age a grasping habit and a determination to have more, or make more, than his brother.

As a young toad in residence at the Hall, Groat caused nothing but trouble and heartache to both his parents and older brother alike and finally left the country rather under a cloud. I believe he fled to North America, taking the family silver with him.

"Even then, and from afar, he sought to contest his brother Toad Senior's claim to the Toad Hall estate, and to wrest from him all his inheritance on wholly specious grounds. A good deal of money was lost by Toad Senior defending himself against this mischievous action.

"When that failed, Groat returned incognito, having learned the arts of agitation and clandestine warfare in America, which is a hotbed of such things, and sought to whip up the weasels and stoats in the Wild Wood to revolution. In fact, he very nearly succeeded in having them advance as a body upon the Town and then on Parliament, bringing scandal and notoriety to the neighbourhood.

"Finally, when the long arm of the law reached out to grasp him – for selling shares in a nonexistent company and persuading many thousands of aged gentlefolk to part with their savings – he was arrested, arraigned and sentenced to twelve years' hard labour in one of our strictest moorland prisons.

"When he was set free he never darkened the door of Toad Hall again, but with a small handout from his ever-generous older brother, who extracted from all who knew about the affair, including myself, the promise never to mention it again, Groat established a business in the north. There, by dint it must be said of a habit of unstinting hard work learned in gaol and wise investment, he became very rich indeed. I believe his wealth increased still further when he set sail back to America, and there invested his money in the railway and steel industry, and latterly, though now very old, in the oil business, as they call it."

"Would that be cooking oil, such as is used in certain of the bigger culinary establishments?" enquired the Mole.

Badger shook his head.

"We are not talking of frying pans, Mole, but of motor-cars. I have heard it said that Toad's Uncle Groat became the richest toad in America, till he returned to his home in the north and retired."

"My!" said the Mole, rather impressed. "But I still don't see how this affects Toad's Christmas."

"You soon will," said the Badger. "I mentioned that after Toad Senior's demise, and some two decades after anybody had heard anything directly from Groat, a telegraphic communication came for Toad from a northern city. By then most folk along the River Bank had forgotten all about Groat – though some of the older weasels and stoats still revered his memory, and practised certain arcane rituals before his effigy in the deeper shadows of the Wild Wood. In fact, I have reason to believe they still do – hence our concern for your safety earlier this evening."

Mole looked anxiously at the windows of the Badger's parlour, where leafless branches fretted at the panes, and he shuddered at the thought of what terrible tortures and cannibalistic practices he might have been witness to, and victim of, had it really been the Wild Wooders who had taken him that evening.

He looked to the Badger to continue the tale, glad of the comfort of the fireside. To tell the truth, the Mole was more thrilled than anything else by what he had heard. He had no idea that Toad had such a colourful relative, and could now better understand why the Badger had always kept such a close eye on Toad's behaviour. It was plain that in that troublesome animal there was as much of his uncle's criminal and revolutionary tendencies as his father's natural goodness.

Badger went on to explain that the telegraph from Uncle Groat announced that Nanny Fowle, formerly nanny to Groat and Toad Senior, and her daughter had fallen on hard times. Groat felt he had a duty of care towards them, and they would therefore be spending Christmas at Toad Hall, and Toad was to see to it *"that every courtesy was extended to them, and no trouble or expense spared."*

Groat added, *"It will do you good to think of others before yourself, which I understand is not a virtue your father ever taught you."*

"That's rich, coming from *him*," murmured Mole.

"By that time, Nanny Fowle was very old, and her daughter was no longer a girl but a woman, and no longer a married woman but a widow. She goes by the name of Mrs Ffleshe."

"With two 'ff's' and an 'e'," murmured the Mole almost without realising it.

"Be that as it may, Mole, Groat's telegraph concluded with these ominous words in reference to Mrs Ffleshe: *'You will not find her in any way difficult or unpleasant provided you accede to her occasional whim and agree at once to opinions she may from time to time feel inclined to express with regard to your domestic arrangements, and upon three subjects in which she believes herself to be something of an expert: religion, politics and members of any sex other than her own, namely those who are of the male gender. On such issues I advise that silence is golden, and the virtue of turning the other cheek is to be practised. I suggest it is not much to ask of you these few days each year, and I know you will find it in your heart to accommodate her in the manner to which she likes to be accustomed.'*

"Toad had never heard of Mrs Ffleshe, but he knew a little of Nanny Fowle, for his father, Toad Senior, used to wake up of a night in a cold sweat crying out her name in terror. Toad was told that she used to lock up his father in the coal cellar without a light as punishment, and steal his nursery food and eat it for herself. On another occasion she took him and Groat into the Village and showed them certain instruments of medieval trial and torture in the Court House there and threatened to use them if they did not behave better and do what she said. Such was Nanny Fowle."

"And this lady and her daughter were those imposed on Toad by Groat?" said the Mole.

"Quite so," said Badger. "People often feel they owe a debt to those who have taken advantage of them. Be that as it may, so many years had passed that Toad, who is by nature generous of heart if often foolish of mind, said he would accept the guests into the Hall and even invited Groat for that same Christmas. He began to grow suspicious, however, when Groat excused himself on rather dubious grounds. Toad then tried to withdraw

his offer of hospitality, but swiftly received another communication, which read like a command. It reminded Toad that he, Groat, was still Lord of the Manor and might if he wished arrest any who did not show him fealty.

"You are probably not aware, Mole, that there is in the Village not only a Court House but a penal institution. Toad was left in no doubt by his uncle where he would be incarcerated if he continued to resist his uncle's request. It was at this point that Toad realised that things were not quite as he had thought and the terrible possibility dawned on him that Groat might dispossess him if he wished.

"In his panic, he hurried here and sought my counsel. We took legal advice and the lawyer unexpectedly suggested that Toad *should* agree to the visit, and for a very disturbing reason.

"'*Having reviewed the papers in this case,*'" said he in a lengthy letter to Toad, "*and studied your Uncle's latest communication, I fear that it appears that with your father's demise he inherits a vestigial, residual and pejorative right of access to Toad Hall, and that as Lord of the Manor and Chairman of the Trustees of his brother's will, he has the casting vote in any determination of its domestic arrangements, offices and income. Since he appears at this stage not to have any wish to exercise that right our advice is not to provoke him, but to accede to his wishes with regard to visitors.*"

This was alarming indeed. It was news to Toad that a trust controlled Toad Hall and that Groat was chairman of it. Further enquiry established that this matter, and

the question of Groat's jurisdiction over Toad Hall as Lord of the Manor and its estate and income, was not quite as certain as his lawyer implied, but clarification would require a lengthy and expensive action through the Court of Protection, probably followed by an appeal before the Judges Inquisitorial – a prospect that naturally terrified the cowardly Toad.

"Such, Mole, were the unhappy circumstances leading up to that fateful first visit of Groat's former nanny to Toad Hall. I will not go into details of how appalling this imposition has been, except to say that if Nanny Fowle was bad, Mrs Ffleshe was far worse, being every host's idea of an interfering, imposing guest.

"Why, I was there myself for dinner when she summoned the Cook and, having berated her in public, dismissed her before Toad could say anything! One year, she turned Toad out of his bedroom, complaining of the

cold in her own, and to my certain knowledge when her friends come a-visiting – which they do at Toad's expense – she banishes him to his old nursery, saying to his face that he is not her social equal and she does not wish to be let down my him."

"Good heavens!" exclaimed the Mole.

"In short, she is rude, grasping, importunate, snobbish, unkind, ungrateful and a bully, and has poor Toad in her thrall. He has become so ashamed of her treatment of him over the years, and of her rudeness to his friends, that five years ago he begged us never to mention her name or her existence."

"Yes, he sat in this very room, Mole, and he wept openly," said the Rat. "He told us that he is powerless to prevent her coming, and unable to stop her behaving as she does. She has now ruined his Christmas for many years and were it not for the loyalty and devotion of his housekeeper Miss Bugle he would long since have departed this life over Christmastide out of sheer misery and exhaustion."

"But this is outrageous!" cried the Mole, rising. "And to think this lady is not even a relative! Something must be done!"

"Do you not think that we agree with you?" said the Badger. "We have racked our brains over the matter and can find no solution that is not criminal and might lead us to the dock. We have honoured our promise to Toad not to mention these matters to others. Yet the fact is that she has ruined not only Toad's Christmas but the Village's as well, for she adamantly refuses to allow him to purchase any seasonal supplies or offer charity in that quarter.

"One year, when he attempted to give money to the Village to make up for this loss of custom, the weasels reported him to her. She told Groat and Groat warned Toad not to do such a foolhardy thing again. 'Charity ends at home' were the words he used, if I remember aright.

"Nanny Fowle has long since passed on, but a pattern has been set and every year Mrs Ffleshe comes to stay for the festive season, often bringing guests whom she wishes to impress, and inviting others to give the impression that she is mistress of Toad Hall.

"Such is Toad Hall's sad festive history in recent years. You were quite right in what you said earlier – there *is* a malaise along the River Bank. The Hall was always the centre of things here and without it the heart has gone out of Christmas, and I believe in the Village as well.

"I confess that it is not helped by the fact that we – that is Ratty and I – are bachelors, and so have no family with whom to celebrate Christmas. We have fallen out of the habit of it. As for Otter here, though he has his son Portly, he does not advertise the fact that Portly's mother departed this area for sunnier climes some time ago."

"I did not mean to pry," said the Mole, much embarrassed by this revelation.

"It's all right, old fellow," said the Otter jovially, "there are plenty of others about who are only too happy to furnish the Otter household with mince pies and suchlike when Christmas comes. That's why I tend to be otherwise engaged at this time of year – fending 'em off! As for Portly, he is spending this Christmas with his mother, which is another reason that I am not much inclined to celebrate: I miss him!"

"O my," said the Mole who now began to see the complexity of the situation. "But at least Mrs Ffleshe's power does not extend to Mole End!"

"Mercifully not. But we felt it best not to trouble you with these matters."

"I thought it was because I had done something to offend you!"

"My dear Mole!" cried the Badger, clapping him on the shoulder. "I am sure I speak for the others as well when I say that your presence amongst us this last year has been a pleasure and a joy, and we would be gravely distressed if you ever thought otherwise. As for your invitation to spend a little time with you over the festive season I for one apologise for my earlier reluctance and if you'll oblige me by asking me again I will accept unreservedly."

"I will oblige, I will!" cried the Mole happily, looking at once to the other two.

"We'll accept as well if you'll have us!" said the Rat and the Otter together.

"I shall send you the invitations tomorrow without fail," cried the Mole.

"Good, then that matter at least is settled" said the Badger. "Now, Mole, it is our tradition, though one that seems very pale when set against what used to happen, to visit Toad on Christmas morning, if only to remind him that he has friends in the outside world. Mrs Ffleshe is invariably rude, and her guests likewise, and poor old Toad is barely allowed to speak to us. We rarely stay longer than a few minutes. After that we retire to one or other of our homes and have a little repast and then go our separate ways, for our spirit is not in it. Perhaps this year…"

"Why, this year you'll come to Mole End and I'll give you a welcome that will keep you with me rather longer than a few minutes!" said the Mole, almost dancing about with excitement and glee.

"We shall be very obliged to you, Mole. Eh, Ratty? Otter?"

They nodded their heads so vigorously, and showed such pleasure on their faces to see the Mole's pleasure, that it seemed for a time that not only were the trials and tribulations of the day quite forgotten, but the bigger problem of Mrs Ffleshe was as nothing too.

Soon the excitement of the day and the lateness of the hour began to take their toll. First, a gentle snoring came from Otter's chair and then the sound of slow breathing from Rat's. Till at last, with a final sigh, Badger rose and retired to the solace of his bed.

Which left just Mole awake, staring at the dying fire and pulling his plaid tighter about his chin but feeling happier than he had for weeks as he planned his menus for the coming Christmas feast and remembered how long it was since he had been honoured to have such company for Christmas. Company he could not better, not better at all, except – except –

"Except for Toad, for he should be there as well, and we *must* see about that," said the Mole. His face hardened with new resolution and he added, "We shall find a way to reinstate the festive season along the River Bank. O hang it! Someone must do something and it seems that someone must be me!"

This much decided, the Mole closed his eyes and fell into sleep, though it was for a long time troubled and restless. But when dawn came the furrows on his brow began to smooth, and a slight smile came to his face, as if he were dreaming of joyous Christmases past, and all the possibilities of happy Yuletides yet to come.

· V ·
Below Stairs

Just as the Mole was the last to go to sleep, so he was the first to awaken, and he did so with a jolt. It was as if a long-unheard but dearly remembered voice had spoken to him, saying, "Prepare in advance and you'll enjoy your guests' coming; prepare too late and you'll be more glad to see their going."

It was his sister's voice he heard, she who had taught him this dictum, and so drilled it into him that he heard it now as if from her own mouth.

He rose stiffly from the depths of the Badger's armchair and decided to complete his ablutions at home rather than disturb his sleeping friends. But he did not leave before he had quietly re-set and lit the fire, and hung a kettle over it, so that they might more easily enjoy a fresh pot of tea when they awoke.

Then, though he had to stand on a chair to reach the uppermost bolt on the Badger's front door, he did so without making too much noise and was off with the rising sun.

When he crossed the Canal Bridge, and then walked back over the Iron Bridge, he saw that the River had calmed down a little, even though its colour was stained by mud and it seemed to have risen further still. He paused for a moment, thinking of all the many things he must do, and heard the unmistakable and ominous sound of the distant Weir.

"Things will get worse and more treacherous before they get better," he said aloud, repeating a phrase that the Rat was fond of using when the River was in change.

But the bright winter sunshine cheered the Mole, as did his memory of the conversation at the Badger's fireside the night before, and the ready affirmation by his friends that he was after all a part of their community. So much so that they had all been willing to change their habits and come to Mole End for a party on the morning of Christmas Day.

"Well, there is no point in waiting around here all day," the Mole told himself, "there's a lot of work to be done..."

Back in the comforting surroundings of Mole End, Mole busied himself with plans for his party, filled with new hope. As always, he had a good supply of food already prepared and safely stored in his larder. It would be nothing more than a morning's work to add the finishing touches, and that he would do tomorrow. In the meantime, there were invitations to write, so he made a pot of tea and sat by his fire with a pen in his hand, enjoying this pleasant task.

He decided to deliver Toad's invitation to Toad Hall that very day. At the same time, he would take along the chestnut and prune compote he had promised to Miss Bugle, and perhaps take the opportunity to ask her help and advice concerning Toad, which would surely be invaluable, if only she could be persuaded to give it.

Finally, when all was ready, the Mole put Toad's invitation in his pocket and the gift for Miss Bugle in a bag and set forth once more for Toad Hall, feeling even more cheerful than before.

Not wishing to cause his friend Toad any unnecessary embarrassment, he took the liberty of knocking at the tradesman's door he had used before. In this way, he also hoped that he would find Miss Bugle without having to engage with Mrs Ffleshe or Toad.

He was extremely surprised, therefore, when the door was answered by none other than Toad himself, dressed in an apron and carrying a knife in one hand and a half-peeled potato in the other.

"Toad! Whatever are you doing?" said the Mole in blank astonishment.

Toad looked greatly relieved to see him and, grabbing him by his lapel, pulled him abruptly into the nearby pantry and shut the back door.

"Mole, O dear, dear Mole!" he cried in a piteous voice. "You should not be here, but now you are, now you are..."

But Toad could say no more.

The knife fell from one hand and the potato from the other and he slumped at the Mole's feet, weeping loudly and crying out, "I cannot stand it another moment. Mrs Ffleshe has given Miss Bugle the morning off and made *me* work here in the kitchen in her place! I can't return upstairs till I have peeled these twelve pounds of potatoes to her satisfaction. She is coming to inspect my work at noon and it is taking so long, so long..."

Toad's tears got the better of him once more and he could only sit at the Mole's feet and weep.

"But, Toad," cried the concerned Mole, picking up the knife and half-peeled potato. "Are you not master of this establishment and able to decide who does the kitchen work?"

"I am, and yet I am not!" whispered Toad. "For fifty weeks of the year I am, and for two weeks I most definitely am not."

"Why don't we talk about it while I help you?" said the sensible and generous Mole, donning an apron that hung from a nearby hook and taking up a second kitchen knife. "After all, twelve pounds of potatoes is not much really. It will take no time at all."

"Not much?" cried Toad, his face brightening.

He rose to his feet and watched admiringly as the Mole began to peel the potatoes with a speed and expertise that came from long practice.

"My word, Mole," cried Toad, taking off his apron and bringing forward a kitchen chair so that he might sit and watch, "you certainly know what you're doing, don't you? But then I suppose that I, Toad of Toad Hall, am accustomed to thinking on a higher plane than vegetables, and with my time and energies so much occupied with the complex affairs of the estate, I cannot seriously be expected to do such work... Goodness me, you really *are* an expert!"

"It's very kind of you to say so, Toad," said the Mole with pleasure, working even harder at Toad's task and unaware of the look of indolent satisfaction that had overtaken Toad's so recently grief-stricken face. "But it wouldn't take me a moment to show you how potatoes should be peeled."

A look of alarm overtook his friend's face.

"No, no!" he spluttered. "Don't let me slow you down, old chap. You've got a good head of steam up, if I may say so, and after all, twelve pounds of potatoes is nothing very much at all. Instead, let me busy myself with the more humble task of finding us both a glass of sherry to keep us busy at our work."

Toad disappeared, leaving the Mole working hard. He tripped gaily down the scullery passage and thence to his wine cellar where he spent not a little time tasting the many fine sherries, finally choosing an excellent *fino,* which he judged just right to keep the Mole at his kitchen work.

By the time he returned, the Mole had as good as finished peeling the potatoes.

"Now," said Toad rather unconvincingly, "you were saying that you might teach me."

"I was indeed," said the Mole, "and I have kept by these last few so that I can show you –"

"The last few?" said Toad, making no move to help his friend Mole. "Won't it be so much quicker if you finish them off yourself and teach me potato peeling another time?"

As the Mole did so, Toad supped his sherry with evident pleasure and continued to bemoan his fate. Then, when the Mole had finished the potatoes, put them in a large pan and covered them with water, Toad suddenly burst into tears once more.

"O, Mole, I am so very wretched and miserable."

"But, Toad," said the perplexed Mole. "Your task is done and it is nowhere near twelve o'clock."

"That is true," whispered Toad brokenly, "but Mrs Ffleshe never does things by halves. I'm afraid I have more vegetables than just a few potatoes to prepare by noon if she is not to confine me to my room for the rest of Christmas."

"Confine you to your room!" cried the Mole, outraged.

"I fear so," said Toad, snivelling mournfully between sips of his sherry. "But you see, Mole, before the force of her indomitable person I am as nothing and I must bend to her will."

"Well, I think you should stand up to her," said the Mole stoutly.

"I might, indeed I might, and I *shall*," said Toad, very unconvincingly. "But only after I have dealt with these Brussels sprouts, which must be made ready for boiling – I suppose it is too much to ask... No, I cannot and will not ask such a thing! I am sure I *can* do these fiddly sprouts if I must, red raw though my fingers are from my earlier work."

Toad made a pathetic show of putting his apron back on.

"My dear friend," said the gullible Mole, "let me at least begin them for you while we decide how to deal with Mrs Ffleshe, for this sort of thing surely cannot be allowed to continue."

"Would you?" said the Toad, brightening once more. "And these carrots, too, which I believe need washing before they are peeled – use that sink over there, old fellow, if you don't mind – after which all we have to do is to clean the floor and hang out the washing and then

– but look how the time is rushing by! Hurry up, Mole, don't dawdle, or else I'll be late!"

Before he knew it, Mole found himself doing the work of several scullery maids whilst Toad, glass in hand, warmed himself by the range, stirring occasionally to give further commands to his too-willing friend.

"Come on, Moly!" he cried as the minute hand of the kitchen clock neared twelve. "She'll be down to make her inspection in a moment. Here, you've forgotten to slice up these cabbages, and be sure to do it neatly, she likes straight lines to her vegetables – no, straighter than that, Mole! I mean to say, if a job's worth doing, it's worth doing well, don't you think?"

"Well, I suppose I do," said the Mole, his patience beginning to wear thin, "but I hope you won't mind if I give Mrs Ffleshe a piece of my mind when she appears."

"A piece of your mind!" cried Toad in alarm. "No, no, no, please do not even think of such a thing. If you spoke out of turn she would punish me all the more."

Just then they heard the ominous sound of someone coming down the stairs from the main house. The steps they heard were heavy and purposeful, with that sharp, jabbing, remorseless quality of a dominant woman on the prowl.

"She's coming," gasped Toad.

"Well, if you won't stand up to her I will!" said the Mole with determination, taking off his apron.

"*Toooad!* Come here at once!" came the sharp command, in that same harsh voice the Mole had heard a day or two before in the company of Mr Baltry.

Mole frowned and said, "Let me go first and I'll tell her –"

"No!" cried Toad in a desperate voice, lunging suddenly at the Mole, grasping him by the shoulder, and frog-marching him backwards. Then, before he could protest, Toad shoved him bodily through the coal-cellar door and shot the bolt.

"Toad, let me out at once!" cried the Mole.

"My life won't be worth living, Moly, if you admonish her!" whispered Toad wildly through the keyhole. "So please keep quiet, there's a good chap!"

"Toad, where have you gone?" boomed Mrs Ffleshe as she reached the bottom stair.

Mole was rather inclined to hammer at the door and make a fuss but his natural courtesy forbade it, and anyway, having already briefly met Mrs Ffleshe, he could understand Toad's dilemma. It would do no good embarrassing him before his ghastly guest.

He heard Toad call out, "Here – I'm here, Mrs Ffleshe, here doing my work." Then in an abject and humble way Toad continued, "And I am so honoured that you have descended below stairs to grace me with your presence, because –"

"Never mind that, Toad," barked Mrs Ffleshe, "the only question is, have you done your work or not? Because if not then I will have no choice but to –"

"But *of course* I've done my work, Mrs Ffleshe," said Toad obsequiously, adding in a sweet, winning voice, "and I have done it happily, reflecting on the errors of my ways, for which you have so rightly chastised me."

Mole applied his eye to the keyhole and watched the proceedings. He saw Toad bow and scrape before the not inconsiderable figure of Mrs Ffleshe, who was arrayed in silks of purple and green, her bosom like the prow of an enemy battleship.

Her face and gaze were severe as she looked down upon Toad. "I wish to examine your work," said she.

Toad pointed smugly at the potatoes that Mole had peeled, the sprouts that Mole had prepared, the carrots that Mole had cleaned and chopped and the cabbage that he had so neatly sliced.

"All done with my own hands," said the brazen Toad, "which are sore and bleeding from the task, but I don't mind, for I deserved it!"

She looked at the vegetables with evident surprise, and then picked up one or two to examine them more closely.

"Hmm, I must say, Toad," said Mrs Ffleshe in a gentler voice, "these are well done, and all the peelings and dirty water cleared away."

"Though I say it myself, Mrs Ffleshe, I am a dab hand at such things," said Toad, who could not resist gilding the lily, "for my Pater, bless him, thought it good for the education of one who would grow up to be a country gentleman that he should learn how the other half lives and works. See how I have been careful to sweep the floor, and dust the range as well."

Mrs Ffleshe nodded her approval and said, "I certainly do see, Toad, and I am glad you have learnt your lesson. Now, come on back upstairs and try to be a good Toad for the rest of the day."

"I will, I will," cried Toad almost gaily. "Ladies first, Mrs Ffleshe, ladies first."

With that, and without a backward glance, the ungrateful Toad disappeared up the stairs and out of sight, leaving the Mole immured in the dark, dank, dingy coal cellar.

For twenty minutes, the Mole waited in silence before he began to realise that Toad was not going to come back down again.

Mole was not easily given to ire, but ireful he now felt.

He began to bang on the door, calling out for somebody to let him out, but no one came. Then he tried to reach up to the circular cast-iron cover above his head, climbing on the coal itself to do so, but he could not quite reach it.

It was perhaps an hour later, his voice by now grown hoarse from shouting, his feet two blocks of ice and his teeth chattering, that he heard the sound of horses' hooves and wagon wheels above his head. He just had time to pull himself upright and look up before the coal-hole cover was removed, and a shaft of daylight nearly blinded him.

"H-h-help!" he called through chattering teeth. "It's Mr Mole of Mole End, and I –"

These words were barely out before the hole above his head darkened and a spatter of coal dust fell on to his face and into his mouth, the only warning he had before half a hundredweight of coal was poured down on top of him.

Mole only saved himself from injury by leaping back against the door, as with a thunderous roar the next load of coal came down, and with it a choking black dust thicker than any he had ever known.

As he began to cough and gasp, light reappeared and he just had time to croak, "Please, no more – I am down here – I –" when the rumbling darkness returned, and another load tumbled down, roaring like an avalanche towards where Mole cowered against the door.

The coal was like a living, growing thing and the Mole soon had to climb and scrabble up to keep himself from being submerged.

"Help!" he croaked as light briefly reappeared.

But the cover was swiftly slid back over the hole and the coalman and his cart soon gone. The Mole supposed that this was a small mercy, for at least no more coal would come down. Now he could only cough and gulp and splutter as he turned to the door and tapped pitifully at its black and gritty surface.

When it finally opened, the poor, suffering Mole tumbled straight out and lay gasping, barely conscious, at the feet of the astonished Miss Bugle, who was brandishing a poker.

"But – but –" she said, "I thought it was mice!"

"Water!" gasped the Mole, who felt he was dying of thirst. *"Water!"*

"I'd better get help at once."

"No," he cried, "no, please do not. Toad will get into trouble, don't you see?"

"But, Mr Mole, I absolutely insist," said Miss Bugle.

"And I absolutely insist you do not," said the Mole very firmly. "Please, if you could just bring me a glass of water and let me warm myself by the range."

Miss Bugle stared at him for a moment and realised that his mind was quite made up.

"Very well, Mr Mole," she said reluctantly, "but as housekeeper of this establishment I should like to know how you got into this predicament. Look at you, you're quite black with coal dust! At least permit me to dust you down."

The glass of water came, and then another, and the solicitous Miss Bugle put the kettle on the range to brew Mole a pot of tea. Then she took him outside into the back courtyard – a precaution he himself insisted on – and began to dust him down with a feather duster.

A great cloud of coal dust flew up in the air, but much of it flew down again – back on to Mole.

"It's not making much impression, I'm afraid," said

the Mole. “Don’t you have a carpet beater?”

“We have, sir,” said she, “but I really think –”

Then the light of realisation came into her eye.

“Goodness, I quite forgot! Some weeks ago, before Mrs Ffleshe arrived, Mr Toad ordered a new cleaning gadget from London. It has not been out of its bag yet, but if I may say so, Mr Mole, in your present state you are the perfect object upon which to try it out!”

Ever afterwards, the Mole preferred to draw a veil over the events of the next hour or so. Suffice it to say that with the brand-new Dustaw Rotary Windsor vacuum cleaner that Toad had so thoughtfully acquired for his housekeeper, and using its finest bristle upholstery brush – and with the Mole lying on the floor and turning the handle himself to create the suction, since Miss Bugle found she could not do both actions at once – that obliging lady successfully managed to vacuum-clean the Mole so that in less than an hour of intensive labour he was, once more, nearly as spick and span as when he first arrived.

Nor was his pride hurt, or good humour affected, for he realised very early on in these dusty proceedings that as a result of this to-do he and Miss Bugle were getting to know each other a great deal quicker and better than a spinster lady and a bachelor Mole might normally be expected to do.

He had soon discovered from Miss Bugle's sharp asides concerning Mrs Ffleshe that she was not one of those retiring spinsters who, like so many of her age and station, was a little too meek and mild for her own good. He saw now that she was made of sterner stuff than he had imagined, and he was sure that she might be – no, she *would* be – an ally in his campaign to bring some general improvements to the River Bank Christmas.

He was about to broach this delicate subject when he remembered the compote he had brought her as a gift. He produced it from his bag with something of a flourish and not a little pride. Though not wrapped in paper, it was brightly ribboned and labelled, and he had written his festive greetings under her name and followed it with his signature.

Her eyes brightened at once, and for a moment he thought they might fill with nostalgic tears. She held it tightly to her bosom, as if to suggest that if she received no other festive gift than this it would be enough to warm her heart and cheer her spirit. Then she said with considerable feeling, "I am glad indeed that Christmas so evidently lives in your heart, Mr Mole, as well as it does in mine, for I swear its expression has very nearly died in this house these past years! Yet not completely, no not absolutely, for I make sure it does not."

"I am glad if you can find some time to celebrate Christmas yourself," said the Mole quietly, "for I rather feared that the responsibilities of having the Hall to organise would prevent you from doing so."

"Well, I should not quite say 'celebrate' in the sense you mean, for Mrs Ffleshe is a demanding guest, if I may put it that way."

Mole murmured that she might if she wished.

"But I always make sure I have the afternoon of Christmas Eve to myself, at least till seven o'clock, and upon this point I have had my way with Mrs Ffleshe. I shall do most of the work I need to this evening so that I can have that time to myself tomorrow afternoon. How very much I look forward to it!"

"I am glad of it, Miss Bugle," returned the Mole, "glad indeed, for I dare say you have no other liberty between now and the sixth of January."

The Mole was about to tackle the subject uppermost in his mind when Miss Bugle stood up in an animated way and interrupted his search for suitable words.

"Twelfth Night!" she cried, eyes brighter still. "How Mr Toad Senior used to make us all enjoy *that* special ritual. 'Miss Bugle,' he would say, 'kindly make sure that not all the decorations are taken down for I like to see the glitter to the end!'

"I would take him at his word, and see to it that those decorations we used to place over the dining room fire, in whose grate the Yule log was first lit, were left till last. Then as the embers died he would summon all the staff from butler down to bootboy, from housekeeper down to under-scullery maid, and he would propose

Mole found himself doing the work of several scullery maids... *(p. 86)*

our health, guests and servants alike. O he was a *jolly* gentleman, Mr Mole!"

"I dare say you miss him still?" said Mole with a smile.

"I do. O I do – but I do not forget him. Why, on Christmas Eve I –"

She paused and looked suddenly a little coy as if she was about to make a revelation she should not. The Mole had the very good sense to remain silent, for he saw that the infectious spirit of Christmas might do his plotting for him.

"Mr Mole," she began impulsively, looking again with pleasure at his gift, "would it be too bold of me to ask if this compote, which I believe you said was of chestnut and prune, might be taken with afternoon tea with clotted cream?"

The Mole said it would go very well with that. He certainly had enjoyed it at tea-time many times.

"You do not quite understand me, Mr Mole. I am sure I should not be so bold, but..."

The Mole smiled as encouragingly as he could.

"Yes, Miss Bugle?" he said with a twinkle in his eye, his heart filled with joy to discover that the spirit of Christmas was not quite dead along the River Bank after all.

"Might I ask if you would be so kind as to be my guest tomorrow afternoon, Mr Mole, because – well, because I would be so very much obliged if you would!"

Mole was very well aware from what she had said earlier what a compliment and honour this was, and nothing, absolutely nothing, could have delighted him more. Why, his social calendar, so empty but two days before, was filling up very rapidly indeed.

"Madam," said he, rising rather formally, "I shall be as honoured as I shall be delighted. Would four o'clock be the correct time for me to arrive? By then dusk will be upon us and I will be less likely to be observed by Mrs Ffleshe or Mr Toad."

"Four o'clock, sir, let it be four o'clock!" cried Miss Bugle gaily.

"I shall look forward to it inordinately, and I will save till then the matter I had come expressly here today to discuss with you. It will be all the better for being mooted over tea!"

"Well then, Mr Mole, let it be so!"

As he took his leave she put her hand on his arm.

"Mr Mole?"

"Madam?"

"Forgive me, but what exactly caused you to be confined in the coal cellar?"

Mole laughed.

"That too can wait, Miss Bugle, for it has a great deal to do with the issue I wish to discuss with you. Suffice it to say, if being half-suffocated by coal dust was the only way I might have had an invitation to tea with you upon Christmas Eve then, madam, I would gladly undergo the ordeal again."

Miss Bugle laughed with pleasure, and the Mole chuckled nearly all the way home.

· VI ·
On Christmas Eve

At the appointed time the following afternoon, wearing a hat to hide his face in case Toad or Mrs Ffleshe caught sight of him, the Mole scurried round the side of Toad Hall and knocked at the tradesman's entrance.

Miss Bugle was ready and waiting. After the briefest but brightest of greetings, she hurried him through the kitchen and, holding a candle to light the way, up the narrow back stairs to the servants' quarters above.

The Mole was not in the habit of surreptitiously making his way to the private apartments of spinster ladies and was both amused and a touch embarrassed to find himself in such a situation. But so too, it seemed, was Miss Bugle.

She bustled up the stairs with an urgency to her step that the Mole guessed came from the fear that if she for one moment hesitated she might not have courage to see her objective through.

When they emerged at last into a corridor on the third floor and turned into the northern wing of the Hall, the Mole found himself so puffed that he had to pause to catch his breath. But Miss Bugle hurried him on till, at last, she brought him before a green door with a polished brass handle.

"Sir," said she with all due propriety, "I realise it is an unusual proceeding for a maiden lady to invite a bachelor into her rooms unchaperoned, but on this special day and in these special circumstances, and in view of what you indicated about your own desire to revive the Christmas spirit by creating some joint plan of action with myself, I feel – I am certain – I hope –"

Her hand went to the handle, but did not yet turn it.

"– that you will understand why I have invited you to tea. I was raised in an orphanage and till I came to the Hall in Mr Toad Senior's day – a happy day for me, most happy! – I had never known a Christmas in a family home. He showed me its joys, and taught me all I know of it. When he passed on –"

The door remained unopened as she continued this personal reminiscence.

"– and Mr Toad's Uncle Groat imposed himself from afar by means of the late Nanny Fowle and Mrs Ffleshe, I fear that something rebelled within me. I decided that come what may I would try to keep the spirit of Christmas alive –"

Miss Bugle began at last to open her door.

"– and just as Mr Toad Senior would have wished me to, and as I believe the present Toad would himself do were he not in thrall to Mrs Ffleshe and ultimately to his Uncle Groat!"

The door opened further.

"Till this moment, Mr Mole, I have never mentioned this matter to a living soul, but when you so unexpectedly offered me the compliments of the season and a gift as well I thought – I felt –"

Miss Bugle could say no more, for the Christmas Eve secret she had held so long was now too much for her to bear and her voice began to break.

"Christmas Eve, Mr Mole, is never a time to be alone, and I have been alone on this day too often. The lights of Christmas candles surely shine brighter in the sympathetic company of others."

"They do, Miss Bugle, O, I know they do!" said the Mole with considerable sympathy and feeling.

"Well then..." she said, pushing her door open with a curious gesture of shy hopefulness and indicating that he should go ahead of her.

What he saw when he entered quite took his breath away. It was a parlour like no parlour he had ever seen. One so filled and resplendent with the Christmas spirit that all the gloom and unhappiness the Mole had recently felt fled from his heart, to be replaced by that sense of simple joy and wonder he had last felt as a child, standing before his first Christmas tree.

From every place that bright Christmas decorations *could* hang, they hung: from the gaslights on the walls, from the central pendant, from the picture rail, from beneath the mantel over the modest fire, from the window latches, from the brass doorhandles, from a hatstand, from the backs of chairs, and from occasional tables – from all of these vantage points, and very many more, there hung shiny silver stars, golden angels, dazzling green fir trees and red Father Christmases.

Some of the decorations simply streamed in shimmering lines, others swooped in handmade chains, and yet others declared themselves as suns and moons, as firebirds, as cherubs, or as reindeers flying through the night. And that was just what hung – for upon every flat surface there were tens, nay hundreds, more decorations, some of wood, some tin, some brass, all brightly coloured or shining, intricately catching the gaslight above and the bright firelight below, and turning it all into a universe of a hundred thousand shimmering stars.

The Mole stood dumbfounded, turning in a complete circle before he moved slowly to the mantelpiece, to reach out and touch a little of what he saw, doing so in pure delight. He had not found such simple pleasure in a festive display since he first saw and touched those wondrous decorations his parents had put up when he was a child.

As then, so now: one moment the world seemed humdrum and normal, the next a door was opened – or rather re-opened – upon the unforgettable glory of bright festive seasonal delight.

Miss Bugle quickly found some tapers to light the candles and their reflections seemed to bring forth a thousand new lights to the festive scene.

"Do you like it?" began Miss Bugle, almost gaily.

"I do like it, I do!" cried the Mole, almost dancing in a circle once again as he surveyed the happy scene, taking in more and more as he did so and feeling the years drop off him in the wonderment of what he saw.

"And this?" he asked, leaning forward to examine a daguerreotype, which was framed with fronds of holly and ivy made most delicately of glass and tin, painted red and green.

"That is Mr Toad Senior and he gave it to me himself at my request. He was too modest a gentleman to think that another might like his portrait. It is my most valued possession. But, Mr Mole, pray be seated by the fireside."

The thoughtful Mole had already observed that there was only one armchair in the room, which was certainly Miss Bugle's own. What need had a maiden lady with no relatives of a second comfortable chair?

At once he went to bring a chair from a dining table that was tucked away in one corner, but when he tried to sit on it Miss Bugle would have none of it, and insisted he take her own. So it was that for a second time in three days, though for very different reasons, the Mole found himself the guest of honour in his host's own chair before a blazing fire. It was a situation that Mole could not imagine being bettered on a Christmas Eve.

It was as well that the compote (his) and the scones and cream (hers) could not be compared because each was sure the other was the better. Nor, had there been a contest as to who was the more sympathetic listener, could one have emerged the victor, for both were undoubtedly experts.

In what seemed like no time at all – though it took a good hour and two pots of tea – Mole had heard the sad story of Miss Bugle's orphan days and learned how Mr Toad Senior had rescued her.

Miss Bugle, in her turn, had wrung from Mole those secrets of his past that bore upon his lost siblings and present regrets that he would not see them again.

"But have you never tried to find your sister's address in the north and make contact with her?" she asked.

He shook his head.

"But, Mr Mole, it is not so very far to those who use the railways!"

"I do not think I would have the courage to do such a thing," said the Mole sadly, "for what must surely be a fruitless search."

With that he let the subject drop. The darkness of the winter evening had fallen as they talked and the Mole became aware that their time was slipping away – soon Miss Bugle would have to resume her duties.

"Mr Mole," said his hostess, "I fear that I have no aperitifs to offer you of the kind that I believe bachelor gentlemen enjoy at this time of evening. I have no brandy or whisky, and certainly no gin! But –"

Mole raised his head hopefully and saw that Miss Bugle had glanced once more towards the portrait of the employer whose memory she revered so greatly.

"I do have a decanter of madeira that was given to me by Mr Toad Senior a very long time ago. There is not much left now, but if you would –?"

Mole indicated that he would indeed, and out came the crystal decanter, accompanied by two exquisitely engraved glasses.

"He gave me these along with the madeira. But up till this moment –"

As she smiled her eyes moistened, and the Mole guessed that till this moment there had never been a reason to fill the second of the glasses, though he noticed it was as brightly polished as the first. No one understood the pleasure of that moment better than he.

"It has been my habit to have a single glass once a year on Christmas Eve, when I toast the memory of those most happy years with Mr Toad Senior."

"Madam," said the Mole, half-rising in alarm, "I cannot think to rob you of a full glass of a drink that is so special, and which I see has now almost run dry. Rather –"

A glance from her stilled him and she filled the glasses without a word, leaving barely enough for two more in the precious bottle.

"Each Christmas Eve I sit here," said she, "and I contemplate my little drink, and I look about at these decorations, which are mainly the Hall's own, for I borrow them from the boxes where they are kept in the attic rooms above, and I ponder the joys of the past year, and such joys as I may find in the year to come. Little did I think that this year would bring into my presence one so gracious and good-hearted as yourself."

She did not yet raise her glass, and nor did the Mole.

"Then I slowly sip my drink and watch the firelight. I think of all those families who have children in their midst, and wonder what they are doing and how excited they must feel…"

"They are inclined to mischief and over-excitement, if my memory of my youth serves me right," observed the Mole with a smile.

Their glasses remained untouched.

"I think too of those who are alone like me, but not lucky enough to have so happy a situation or so benign an employer as the present Mr Toad, and I wish them better luck in the months and years ahead.

"So do the moments of my little Christmas celebration pass. Then, reluctantly, I come to my final task. As the hour of six rings out from the Village church – and when the wind is in the west as it is tonight I can hear it from my open window – I take down these decorations one by one, and pack them up for another year into those wooden boxes you see beneath my dining table. Then I silently transport them back up to the attic whence they came. By that time it is nigh-on seven o'clock and I have to be on duty once again. Then is my Christmas done, even before it has begun for the rest of the world!"

Miss Bugle was silent, and seemed neither happy nor sad, but rather resigned to this solitary annual ritual.

Breaking her silence at last, she said, "I would be very

grateful, Mr Mole, if this year you would be kind enough to propose a toast, for I believe that is a gentleman's prerogative."

"I will do so with great pleasure, madam," said the Mole, who had been much moved by her words. He rose up and declared, "It is my firm belief that this will be the last time that the River Bank's Christmas will be blighted and I am confident that the spirit of Christmas will win through again. I now feel that in you I have the staunchest possible ally for certain efforts I am planning with the help of Mr Badger and others on the River Bank's behalf, and so I feel emboldened to propose the health of Christmas now and for always! May all our wishes regarding it come true!"

Their glasses clinked merrily in the firelight.

They talked a little more in general terms before the Mole felt the moment had come to ask her about something that had nagged at him since Mr Baltry the poulterer had mentioned it, and which had been referred to indirectly by all those he had spoken to since.

"Please answer me this, Miss Bugle, for I believe you are best placed to do so. I have been told that Mr Toad's malaise at Christmas time, and his inability to deal firmly with Mrs Ffleshe, if I may so put it, has something to do with his father. I feel that if I am to take successful action and gain Toad's help, I need to understand Mr Toad's state of mind. Can you cast any light on the matter?"

Miss Bugle nodded her understanding and said very sombrely, "The long and short of it is that Mr Toad's father passed away at Christmas."

"Yes, that much I had discovered," responded the Mole sympathetically

"But did you know it was on Christmas Day itself!" she added tragically. It was plain from the play of emotion upon her face and the passion of her voice that this memory was still very real and fresh in her mind.

"O my goodness!" said Mole with a look of dismay, for this important detail had been omitted from Badger's account.

"I believe that no son loved his father more than Mr Toad Junior loved Mr Toad Senior. The two were quite inseparable, you know, and for Toad Junior the spirit of Christmas *was* his father. Which for anyone honoured to know that gentleman, his good nature, his high spirits, his generosity in all things and his happy knack of putting others at their ease, is scarcely surprising. Why, if he had been *my* father, I believe I might have found it very hard indeed to celebrate Christmas knowing that he had passed away on that day of all days. So it was that with the death of his father, something of the spirit of Christmas also died in Mr Toad's heart."

Miss Bugle shook her head sombrely, the colours of Christmas bright about her.

"Sir, I have striven for years to think of a way of shaking Mr Toad out of his malaise. Indeed, sir, I may say that I have made it my ambition to play a part, however small, in bringing back to Toad Hall the Christmas spirit it has lost. When you suggested that perhaps we might endeavour to do something towards that together my heart was filled with new hope and so – here we now are!"

"Madam," said the Mole, "I am most encouraged by

your words. We shall – we must – find a way to help our mutual friend, in which enterprise I believe we shall be helping the whole of the River Bank! But there is one more thing."

"Ask it, sir!" cried Miss Bugle. "Let us be entirely frank with one another."

"Well –" began the Mole diffidently, for he felt a little guilty that his curiosity on a particular point so troubled him, "it was simply that neither you nor Mr Badger has actually explained to me what caused Toad Senior to pass away and I wondered if that was in any way –"

"His demise was caused by a surfeit of plum pudding."

For a moment the Mole thought he had not heard aright, but he saw from Miss Bugle's seriousness that it was exactly what she had said.

"He choked then…?" suggested the Mole. "Perhaps on a stone?"

"Choked?" repeated Miss Bugle distractedly. "On a stone? I think not. No, he was laughing at the time, you see. O it was terrible, and so unexpected. Everybody was in the banqueting room, the fire cheerfully roaring, his friends all about, the tree glorious with candlelight, listening to Mr Toad Junior making his first festive speech. When he had finished, Mr Toad Senior arose to respond in like manner, saying as he did so, 'I'll have one more mouthful of Cook's plum pudding and I had better make it my last!' Then a spasm of pain passed across his face, and then a look of comprehension as he repeated the fateful word 'last' and began to laugh."

"Laugh?" said the Mole, rather hollowly, for he was not quite sure how to respond.

"Well, they were all laughing, as I remember," said Miss Bugle, "for they did not quite realise the situation. Then suddenly Mr Toad Senior clutched at a cracker, waved it about his head and slumped breathless into a seat by the fire."

"By the fire," murmured the Mole.

"He had begun to recover after his thoughtful son offered him a glass of champagne when he clutched at his chest and fell back once more. Then he bravely managed to cry out 'Merry Christmas!' and, offering one end of the cracker to his son, he was suddenly..."

"Suddenly what?"

"No more," announced Miss Bugle.

"No more?" murmured the Mole, thinking it was as good a way to go as any, and better than most.

"He was gone," said Miss Bugle with finality. "I could see that my employer was now the *late* Mr Toad. And yet… yet…"

"Yes, Miss Bugle?" said the Mole very seriously, leaning forward in a way that perhaps conveyed to her his deep engagement in the story she told.

"Yes," she continued in a softer voice. "He looked very cheerful with a paper hat on his head, a cracker in one hand and a glass of champagne in the other and the firelight on his face. He looked very cheerful indeed. But there was no doubt that his spirit had departed."

"Departed," whispered the Mole, who had some difficulty in picturing the scene without wondering what he might have done in such a situation, had he been a guest at Toad Senior's table. Death he had known, but not death on Christmas Day, the company full of jollity.

Since Miss Bugle remained silent he felt he should say something. But what?

"I think I know," he said finally, and for lack of anything more profound, "what I might have done when faced by such a crisis."

"What would that have been?" asked Miss Bugle with very real curiosity, for she often wondered if she had done the right thing herself.

"I would have removed the paper hat from his head," said the Mole, adding after some thought, "and I think the cracker from his hand."

"That would have been the right thing," concurred Miss Bugle, "always assuming that the cracker would come easily. However, it seemed to me that Mr Toad was holding on to it very tightly and, of course –"

"Yes," whispered the Mole, who knew a little about rigor mortis, and how swiftly it can set in, "it might well have been unseemly to attempt to break his grip."

He said no more, for it was too distressing to contemplate the possible consequences of attempting to pull a Christmas cracker with one who was already deceased and whose grasp was involuntarily growing stronger by the second.

Miss Bugle said, "Yet I wish I or someone else had thought of removing his paper hat before the undertaker came, for they didn't think to do it either. So it was that the undertakers portered Mr Toad out of the dining room with the green paper hat upon his head and the unpulled cracker still in his hand."

Mole sat in silence for a time pondering Toad Senior's distant passing. This information certainly put into a very different light the nature of Toad's festive malaise. The time was right to propose another toast, and this time it was Miss Bugle who proposed it.

"To the memory of Mr Toad Senior and to the final victory of the Christmas spirit!" cried Miss Bugle impulsively, and with such abandon that it seemed possible to the Mole that a single glass of madeira was the equivalent to Miss Bugle of several casks to those more used to alcoholic beverage.

"To victory!" cried the Mole in loud response, to whom it seemed that the image of Mr Toad Senior upon the mantelpiece, and that of several Father Christmases all about, were one and the same, and each one a stalwart party to their shared purpose and revolutionary intent.

"Let's finish off the madeira," said Miss Bugle rather too loudly, and the Mole saw that she was not to be denied, "and then we shall make some plans!"

The two huddled forward in their chairs in the manner of conspirators and agreed that each would do all they could over the next few days to find a way to release Mr Toad from his bondage to the past, in the belief that by doing so they would be helping to free the River Bank.

Later, with the servants' bell now sounding angrily to summon Miss Bugle from far below, she and Mole set about the sad but necessary task of packing up the decorations and carrying them up to the attic till finally, their work done, Miss Bugle closed the attic door behind them.

"You had better use the servants' entrance again, Mr Mole, in case she sees you," advised Miss Bugle. "Good night, Mr Mole."

Thus Mole took his leave and, with so much to think upon, barely noticed that the night was blowing up a storm as he walked across the fields to his familiar front door. Once safely inside, he lit a candle and poured himself a glass of his famous sloe and blackberry. But no sooner had he settled down in the comfort of his own armchair than he heard a whispering at his front door, and a timid knock.

"The field-mice! The field-mice have come a-carolling – Christmas is truly here!" he cried, as he leapt to his feet and hurried to the door to let them come tumbling in – shy, talkative, laughing and finally singing out their Christmas songs.

Mole warmed some mince pies and handed round some fruit punch. Then he told them some stories of his childhood, and yielded to their demands to hear how he and Mr Badger and the Water Rat and the great Mr Toad had once wrested Toad Hall back from the weasels and stoats.

Till at last, when their parents came by to take them home, Mole's Christmas Eve was nearly done.

Yet not quite.

He still had to propose the final toast of the night. He opened his front door and raised his glass to such stars as he could see. "To the memory of my family," said he, "to my parents long gone, to my sister long lost, and my errant brother rarely found. And to my nephew, who I have never met. Wherever they may be, may the

Christmas spirit be with them in the festive days ahead and bring them health and happiness, and contentment." He paused a moment, as the swirling clouds opened up to reveal the moon and stars more clearly than before.

Mole stared and wondered at what he saw and remembered someone he would like to see again.

Meanwhile, far off, further away in the wide world than the Mole had ever been or hoped to go, and as bells ancient and modern rang in a new Christmas, there was another who watched the moon, and saw the stars, and thought of Mole.

"Merry Christmas, my dear," said Mole's lost sister to the distant night, tears in her eyes, "a *very* Merry Christmas, wherever you may be."

Nor, in those wishes, was she quite alone. For just across the fields, the candles in her parlour now nearly all gone out, Miss Bugle also stared out from her window, and watched the moon's brief show.

She whispered a Merry Christmas to the world and impulsively, in the same breath as she mentioned the Mr Toads, Senior and Junior, she dared to add the name of Mr Mole, who had given her so much pleasure that afternoon, and renewed her faith in Christmases past, present and future.

"May his wishes all come true," she said.

She did not close her window till long after the bells of the Village church had ceased to chime.

"I wonder –" she whispered as she blew out the last of the candles in her parlour, "I wonder if I dare!"

The very last candle she blew out, as was her wont, was the one by the image of Mr Toad Senior. He seemed to wink at her, encouragingly, and laugh with all the good humour of the world.

"I could do it," she whispered, "and I *shall*! Not today, which is Christmas, nor tomorrow, which is Boxing Day, but the day after that, when all opens up again. Then – *I will!*"

· VII ·
The Final Straw

Toad of Toad Hall awoke early, with that feeling of despondency and dread he had come to associate with Christmas morning. Not least because it was such very hard work doing the right thing in a house ruled by Mrs Ffleshe, where doing the wrong thing seemed almost inevitable.

The plain fact was that for Toad to survive these twelve long days of Christmas each year he had to be other than he truly was. That glorious triumphant other self, a Toad full of courage, a Toad filled with purpose, a Toad who was the originator and avid proponent of bold schemes far beyond the imaginings of lesser mortals (as Toad perceived it), did not for those twelve days exist.

Nor, come to that, did that vain, conceited, foolhardy, maddening and foolishly generous creature whom the River Bankers knew and loved.

In the place of these two toads, who lived side by side for something more than three hundred and fifty days a year, there was a defeated Toad, a ground-down Toad, a Toad overcome by a torrent of harsh words, a Toad flattened by a female steamroller of abuse and contempt, a wan and pallid Toad; a toad, in fact, who was not *Toad* at all.

How this had come about, Toad himself had long since forgotten, and ceased to concern himself with, for to do otherwise was to cause himself distress, and misery. His only consolation was that but for their brief audience on Christmas morning his friends did not have to see him in this sorry state.

So it was that this Christmas morning Toad rose wearily from his bed, bedraggled in appearance and all but defeated in spirit. He expected nothing of the world that day, nothing at all.

He did not, for example, bother to glance at the bedpost at the end of his bed to which, in happier times, as a child and sometimes as an adult, the Christmas spirit had somehow attached a bulging stocking.

Certainly he did not look out of his window as he had as a child (and, indeed, for all his adult years till the coming of the dreaded Mrs Ffleshe), to see if it was to be a white Christmas and he might go sledging or skating.

He did not even peer into the mirror above his fireplace

before he commenced his ablutions and whisper, however pathetically, "A Happy Christmas, old chap!"

Toad simply groaned and then, sighing, set about preparing himself for the doleful day, his thoughts entirely concerned with how he might contrive to see as little as possible of Mrs Ffleshe, and whatever ghastly guests she had coming that day.

He had to appear at breakfast, that was certain; and luncheon as well. Whether or not he would have to attend dinner depended entirely upon whether or not Mrs Ffleshe had decreed that it was then or at luncheon that they had their Christmas fare. If at lunch, he might avoid evening dinner, so that was his preference, but naturally he was not informed till the last moment.

There was one ritual, however, that he observed with that small part of his spirit Mrs Ffleshe had failed to subjugate – an act of rebellion that took place early in the morning. Mrs Ffleshe had always insisted that Toad should not begin his own breakfast till she had made her appearance, which she normally did some time between nine and ten o'clock. Toad had observed this stricture for a number of years but tended to become rather hungry and ill-tempered by the time Mrs Ffleshe came down, for Toad liked his food and felt faint if he did not have it in good time. The excellent Miss Bugle had circumvented this distressing problem, however, by laying out for him a light repast in the library, where she also lit a fire for him and made sure he had some tea.

This repast, which consisted of porridge in the Scottish manner, a coddled egg or two, some toast and marmalade, and some cooked fruits and fresh cream –

just enough, in short, to keep Toad alive till breakfast – was the quietest and most pleasant part of Toad's long Christmas Day.

The reason Mrs Ffleshe had not put a stop to it was that she generally did not set foot in the library at all. This room, more than any other, had been Toad Senior's retreat. He had banished Nanny Fowle from it and as a consequence her daughter Mrs Ffleshe continued to feel uncomfortable there. Moreover, above the fireplace hung a splendid portrait of Toad Senior at his jolliest and most cheerful, which she could not abide.

Toad would sit under this benign image, aware of the fact that his time was short, and enjoy his pre-breakfast, wondering how on earth he was going to survive the twelve long days of Christmas.

"Never was there a toad unhappier than I, Pater," he would say, as he pondered how much milk to add to his porridge, "for I remember things as they used to be and can never be again." Then, adding some cream to the porridge on top of the milk and tucking in, he continued: "Pater, what can I do but accept my fate? I am a tragic toad, unloved and all alone, for with your passing there is nobody left to care for me."

Then, having finished the porridge Miss Bugle had so lovingly made for him, and engaging with the coddled eggs by way of a pinch of salt and a peck of fresh pepper (freshly ground by Miss Bugle), he glanced up at his father's image, sudden tears streaming down his face.

"O Pater!" he cried, checking that Miss Bugle had buttered his toast as she usually did and seeing that she had, "I am the Wounded King of the River Bank!"

His Pater, had he been able, might well have raised his eyebrows at this comparison but he need not have waited long for an explanation. Polishing off the last of the eggs and gratified to see that there were a good few pieces of toast left over, enough to account for most of the jar of marmalade, Toad added with a certain irony, "A Wounded King, yes, but with no knights to fight his cause, no! There is no one who can rid me of this pestilent woman! She is my fate, my doom and I shall breathe my last before she does, Pater!"

The hour of nine struck and Toad knew he must finish his little meal and join Mrs Ffleshe for breakfast. The only bright spot he had to look forward to in the hours and days ahead was the brief visit of Badger and the others later that morning. This was a tradition he had not permitted Mrs Ffleshe to put a stop to, albeit she complained loudly about it the day before and for several days afterwards, calling his friends "lower-class spongers" and "liberal no-gooders" and "layabout loungers" and several more permutations of the same.

He rose, he looked sadly at his father's eyes and he made his way to the chilly confines of the breakfast room, there to await Mrs Ffleshe's arrival.

"Toad! You are late! You have kept me waiting and I am fainting with hunger. This is not the behaviour of a gentleman, or of one who should be thinking of my happiness and welfare upon Christmas Day!"

The startled Toad stood upon the threshold of the breakfast room in mental disarray. She was early! She was never early without there being a reason that would be to his disadvantage and discomfort. So she had finally invaded even this precious time.

"Kindly do not wish me a Merry Christmas," said the enraged Mrs Ffleshe, "for you have made it begin badly, very badly indeed."

"I am sorry –" began Toad meekly.

"Where have you been?"

"I have – I mean – I was –" stuttered Toad, wondering if there was any coddled egg on his morning jacket, or evidence of porridge on his cuff.

"Well?" she said, rising and staring down at him.

It was at moments like this that she terrified him, for she was bigger than he was and a great deal stronger. At such moments he felt like a naughty child again, that same child who used to be admonished by her mother Nanny Fowle, then already ancient:

"Master Toad, stand up straight!"

"Master Toad, sit down!"

"Master Toad, how dare you presume to have any pudding before you have eaten your meat!"

"Well?" said Mrs Ffleshe, bending down to look into his eyes.

"I –" gasped poor Toad.

"I know where you were. *I know!*"

"O dear," said Toad's inner voice, "she has discovered even this last secret and is about to take it from me. It seems I have just had my final Christmas pre-breakfast in the library. Pater, what shall I do?"

"Mr Toad," said Mrs Ffleshe, rising to her full height, "despite your ill-treatment of me, and your ingratitude for all I have done, I have a present for you – no, I say again it would be distasteful for you to wish me a Merry Christmas now! Here is your present, so be good enough to open it."

More confused than ever, Toad took the square, large, heavy and flat gift from her, before asking, "Might I perhaps have a little breakfast first?"

"Well!" she exclaimed with every appearance of disappointment. "Since your stomach is obviously larger than your gratitude, I suppose you must! When you do finally deign to open it, perhaps you would find time to thank me for my trouble!"

Mrs Ffleshe sat down once more and tucked into her bowl of fat sausages and black pudding, affecting to ignore Toad, who stood before her, helpless and uncertain.

"I suppose…" quavered Toad.

She swallowed some tea.

"I suppose I might..."

She helped herself to half a dozen extra rashers of bacon.

"I – I shall open it now, then," said Toad.

She gazed at him with the smug look of the victor.

"It would certainly be polite to do so," she said acidly.

He tore at the string and paper with sinking heart, for her presents were never things he wanted, and usually things that provoked gloominess in one way or another.

From the shape and feel of it, it was a picture of some kind. Affecting interest and pleasure, but feeling only dread, he tore off the final layer of crepe paper and saw that it was more than a picture, it was a portrait. More even than that, it had been executed in oils which, despite the care with which they had been applied, and the artist's search for colours and a technique that might soften the subject, could not disguise the fact that the subject of the portrait did not have a visage that lent itself to the plastic arts.

"Why, it is a painting of Nanny Fowle!" exclaimed Toad with feigned delight. "How – how –" but words failed him, and after placing it on the sideboard where they could both see it, he studied it bleakly. The thin mouth, the cadaverous cheeks, the straggling hair, the mean and hateful eyes, the pendulous ears, the perpetual frown.

"It is a very good likeness," he said, thinking that he might put the wretched picture in the attic, underneath the skylight that leaked.

"I am glad you like it," she said. "It is for the library."

This was a command, not a statement.

"You want to put it in the library?" spluttered Toad. "But..." A grim thought occurred to him. His father had stressed time and again that the library was the one place Nanny Fowle had never been permitted to go in *any* circumstances. "I rather think – I greatly fear –"

"Yes, Toad?" said Mrs Ffleshe, leaning towards him.

"I don't believe there is quite enough room for it in the library," he squeaked.

"O yes there is," she said with that resolution he knew so well.

He dared say no more to her on the subject, but for the rest of their breakfast he could think of nothing else and quite lost his appetite.

"Not the library, not my Pater's beloved room, not that!" he whispered to himself as Mrs Ffleshe tore at her toast, guzzled her tea and rang imperiously for more of everything. "Not the one place where Pater could escape from Nanny Fowle!"

Mrs Ffleshe rang the bell again and told Miss Bugle that she was slow and the eggs were overcooked and might she please make sure in the days ahead that there was more coal on the fire and that the hot water in her bedroom was not quite so hot but that the towels were a little more warmed.

"Come on, Toad!" said Mrs Ffleshe, rising when her breakfast was over. "I am going to have to suffer your common guests within the hour, so let us hang my mother's portrait before they arrive."

There was nothing for it but to do as she asked.

"Well, Toad, bring it with you then, for goodness' sake! Really, I sometimes wonder..."

He followed reluctantly and found her in the centre of the library, apparently examining the walls and picture rail for the best location.

"You see," he said meekly, "there is no room."

"Then *that* will have to come down!" she cried, pointing at his father's portrait.

"Pater's portrait!" he stuttered, utterly appalled.

It had never occurred to him that she could propose such a thing. Some distant will to fight arose in him and he darted in front of the fireplace to put himself between the picture he loved so much and her large self.

"Mr Toad," she boomed, "I really must insist you take down that picture."

"No!" he gasped, picking up the poker. "I will not – you cannot – I do not –"

"Such ingratitude on Christmas Day!" cried Mrs Ffleshe indignantly before, ignoring his plaints, she pushed him aside and grasped at his father's portrait.

He leapt up and hung on to her arm.

"Unhand me, Mr Toad, or I shall summon the constabulary!" she cried, leaving the picture where it was and stepping back a pace or two, with Toad swinging from her arm like a light pendant in an earthquake.

"Leave it, madam, for if you do not – if you do not –"

"Yes, Mr Toad, *yes?*"

"Then I must – I shall – I –"

It was only when this unseemly struggle had gone on for some moments more that both of them realised that someone had entered the room. It was the Mole and the Badger, who had come ahead of Rat and Otter.

"Ahem!" said the Mole uncertainly. "A very Merry Christmas to you both!"

Mrs Ffleshe fell back at once, as bullies usually do when thus discovered, and with Toad panting hard she said, "Sirs, you are just in time to save me from this brute! Unhand me again I say, Mr Toad, unhand me!"

The Badger was not fooled and nor was Mole.

When there had been no response to their knocks at the front door they had let themselves in and so had witnessed the struggle of the portraits almost from the beginning. Both knew the portrait of Toad Senior very well indeed and how much Toad valued it, and could easily guess how he must feel at the prospect of its being displaced by Nanny Fowle on this day of all days.

"Unhand me, Mr. Toad, or I shall summon the constabulary!" *(p. 126)*

"We have not met formally," said Mole in measured tones and in the absence of any word from the Badger.

She advanced upon him and eyed him much as she had eyed the goose on the day they had met. For one dreadful moment he thought she was going to apply thumb and forefinger to his thigh and arm to see how much meat he had on him, and sniff him too perhaps.

"Don't I know you?" she enquired.

"I am Mr Mole of Mole End, and with Mr Badger here I have come to pay seasonal respects to Mr Toad, and to say that two of our friends, namely Mr Water Rat and Mr Otter, are delayed. They have to –"

"It doesn't matter why they can't come," she said sharply. "You I know, Mr Badger, for you have come along on previous Christmas mornings, have you not?"

"I have, madam. A Merry Christmas to you!"

"Humph!" she said. "You cannot stay long, for we have a luncheon party starting at noon and friends of some social standing will be arriving at that time and I would prefer they did not see people of your station here. I'll give you quarter of an hour, Toad, and then…"

She glared fiercely at them all and departed, leaving behind Nanny Fowle, who stared at them malevolently from where she had been propped.

Toad collapsed into an armchair, head in his hands.

"O calamity!" he groaned. "It is even worse this year than last. I wish you had not seen what you did. By myself I can survive, but knowing you are so near and – and what is worse I locked you in that coal-hole, Mole, and didn't even come to let you out! I feel ashamed in all directions!"

"Toad," said the sympathetic Mole, "there is no need to apologise. Today is Christmas Day and I have come to present these modest gifts to you, which I thought might give you pleasure and solace in the days ahead."

He produced a basket of delicacies and fruit, and one or two other small things all wrapped up and neatly labelled "To Toad" and "For Toad" and "From Mole to Toad".

"Please take them, Toad."

Toad did so with trembling hands, greatly moved. This was not a vain Toad, or a puffed-up Toad, but rather a wan and troubled Toad who had been reminded again, as often before, that it was from River Bankers like Mole and Badger that true friendship came.

"Also, I have an invitation for you to an At Home I am planning later this morning," continued the Mole, "though if you are otherwise engaged –"

A dreadful look crossed poor Toad's face at the prospect of luncheon at the Hall.

"– if you *are* engaged," continued the thoughtful Mole, "then do please come over to Mole End the moment you are free; night or day you will be welcome. Please say you will."

But Toad did not speak. He could only stare at the fire and at the portrait of his father, now askew, and clasp the Mole's basket to his lap as if it were the nicest, kindest gift he had ever had.

But speak? That he could not do. Nor suddenly could his friends.

How long they stayed thus would be hard to say, but they remained so till Miss Bugle knocked on the door and brought in a tray of tea and mince pies. As they tucked in, they could hear Mrs Ffleshe in another room making plain that she thought it time that Toad's guests left, for hers would soon be arriving.

Miss Bugle dared close the library door upon this unseasonal cacophony, as the Mole and the Badger poured tea for Toad, and tried to comfort him.

It was some time later, when Toad was somewhat fortified and seemed to be on the road to recovery, that something happened which seemed to bring to a head all his years of failing struggle with Mrs Ffleshe.

He had finally found enough strength to raise a third cup of tea to his lips when with a slide and crash his father's portrait, which must have worked loose, fell on to the mantel, and from there towards the ground.

In fact, it did rather more than that. It was in a heavy gilded frame and a corner of this crashed unerringly into the portrait of Nanny Fowle and dealt as severe a death blow as can be dealt to an inanimate object. It seemed to tear the portrait apart, frame and all, leaving it in tatters on the carpet, made subjugate by Toad Senior, who quite unharmed smiled benignly at them all, and particularly at his son.

For a long time Toad stayed mute and dumbstruck. Then, suddenly, he decided to take this accident as a sign from beyond the grave – or more accurately a call to action. But to what action, to what purpose?

"I am undone and broken, the wreck of the Toad I once was," he cried, leaping up and scattering tea cups and presents everywhere. "It is my fault! All is lost! The Hall and the River Bank are ruined and I am to blame, for I can never be my father's son!"

"Badger, perhaps you should fetch him a glass of water," said the sensible Mole.

"Water?" cried Toad, turning and turning about in his distress. "What can water do against the awful might of Mrs Ffleshe? Niagara Falls would not trouble her nor a regiment of Hussars subdue her! Arsenic would be as ambrosia to such a one as she, and a stake in the heart would merely be taken as encouragement. No, the combined force of the Roman and Protestant churches could not make her know the meaning of generosity and kindness, and now this has happened to the portrait of Nanny Fowle my life is not worth living. And it is all *my* fault for not standing up to her!"

"Toad!" cried the Mole, who was finding it very hard

to hold his friend down. "Toad, please try to be calm, because –"

These, never a wise choice of words with the excitable Toad, were the very worst just then.

"Calm!" cried Toad, throwing the Mole back against the fireplace and rushing for the door. "I cannot and will not and must not and shall not be calm!"

"Sir!" cried Miss Bugle, who appeared at that moment with the Badger. "Try this – or this!"

She offered him a glass of water with one hand and attempted to waft a bottle of smelling salts under his nose with the other.

"There is no other solution now!" he said, muttering more to himself than them. "Farewell, Miss Bugle! Farewell, Badger! Farewell, my home!"

Rushing to the great front door, he pulled it open violently and found himself facing the party of Mrs Ffleshe's guests, who were just then arriving and who, judging by the cut of their shoes and coats, and the imperiousness of their gaze, were very important personages indeed.

"Farewell to you all," he cried inclusively, knocking them all back down the steps they had just come up. "For now I must leave you and my home for ever!"

With that, he set off across his lawn at a fast pace, heading straight towards the swollen River.

"Quick, after him!" shouted the Mole. "He intends to jump in and he will not survive in such a flood! Badger, try to catch him for you are faster than I, while I make haste to the Iron Bridge and alert Otter and Rat, who are working there."

Without another word, the Badger did as the sensible Mole suggested, calling after Toad and begging, ordering, *demanding* that he stop.

But it was too little, too late, and with hardly a pause in his progress the overwrought Toad ran down to the bank near his boathouse and with a despairing cry flung himself into the flooding waters.

Naturally, this spurred the Badger on still more and though he was by no means a competent swimmer he knew that if he had to he would risk his own life by diving in after Toad.

Meanwhile, Mole had hurried out of Toad's gates and was running as fast as he could towards the Iron Bridge, where he knew that Otter and the Water Rat were carrying out some repairs to damage caused by the weasels and stoats. When he arrived, he was in a state of exhaustion, so breathless that he could only cry out to

Rat, "It's Toad! He's in the…" before pointing upstream.

At that same moment they heard Badger's shouts and saw him standing on Toad's lawn, pointing at the swirling, rushing waters, and they deduced at once that the worst had happened.

"Can you see him?" called the Otter, who was on the bank below.

The Rat was still, staring grimly upstream at the raging waters, eyes travelling from one side to another, from ripple to wave, from swirl to turning current.

"Get the boathook, Otter," he cried, "and pass it up to me. If he surfaces it'll be me who sees him first. I'll try and arrest his passage. There he is! *There!*"

Mole certainly would not have recognised what Rat was pointing at. It looked like a log, or perhaps a scruffy branch as it turned, but then he saw a hand.

"It's Toad!" cried the Mole.

Rat tore off his jacket and leapt over the railings into the water. The current was so strong that the Mole saw at once he would not be able to swim against it to reach Toad, but Rat knew his work, and Otter understood the strategy.

That sturdy animal deftly passed the great boathook to the Rat as he was swept past and then dived in himself and quickly had Toad's inert body in his firm grasp. Meanwhile, downstream the Rat had used the boathook to haul himself to the bank, and he now stood ready to haul in Otter and Toad when they came past.

They did not have to wait long to discover if Toad was still breathing, for moments after Otter had brought him to the surface, Toad began to talk.

"Unhand me! Let me float away to my fate! Let me sink to my Shangri-La! Leave me!"

"O Toad, do be quiet and keep still till we have you back on the bank, or else I *shall* let you go!" gasped the Otter as he strained to pull their struggling friend to safety.

"There's no law in the land to stop a gentleman from going for a swim on Christmas Day!" cried Toad, who seemed suddenly light-headed.

"Push him this way a little, Otter!" cried the Rat from the bank. "That's it!"

Then he expertly hooked Toad by his shirt collar and with the Otter's help heaved him to safety.

"Liberty was so near that I saw its golden beams!" cried Toad as he slumped wetly on to the grass and the others gathered round. "But now – now – I feel a terrible chill upon me, and my limbs are growing numb!"

With that he began to shiver, and his teeth began to rattle, and they judged it best to get him home to bed as swiftly as they could. The resourceful Rat took up one of the larger planks he kept under the bridge for the purpose of shoring up the bank and together they laid the bedraggled Toad upon it. Then, sharing the weight between them, as if they were a funeral cortege and he the corpse, they carried Toad the short distance up the public road to his gates and thence across his drive to his front door.

"The Master's drownded!" cried the stable boy, who had come to see what the fuss was about. "Drownded, soaked and sopping and – by the look of 'im – it's all too late for the doctor!"

This alarming pronouncement brought the household staff outside, where many took off their hats and caps, bowed their heads in grief, weeping openly at the sight of the prone Toad.

A very different diagnosis was made by Toad's long-suffering friends, who concluded that there was nothing much wrong with Toad that a warm bed, a hot drink, some good food and a fire would not soon put right.

"But – but –" cried Mrs Ffleshe, who having shown her guests into the drawing room after Toad's sudden departure now suffered the embarrassment of having them all come out again to see what the fuss was about.

"There are no buts about it, Mrs Ffleshe," said the Badger, taking charge. "The master and, I believe, owner of this establishment, has suffered a slight accident and needs to rest, and I intend to see that he does."

"Sir!" said Mrs Ffleshe, barring their way. "You are a brute to speak to a lady so!"

"Madam!" said the Badger, "I command you to get out of our way or I shall be forced to conclude that the only brute in this establishment is of the female gender!"

"How dare you, sir!" said she, but back away she did, and in they went, with Miss Bugle following, leaving Toad's tormentor and her guests fuming by the door.

· VIII ·
Councils of War

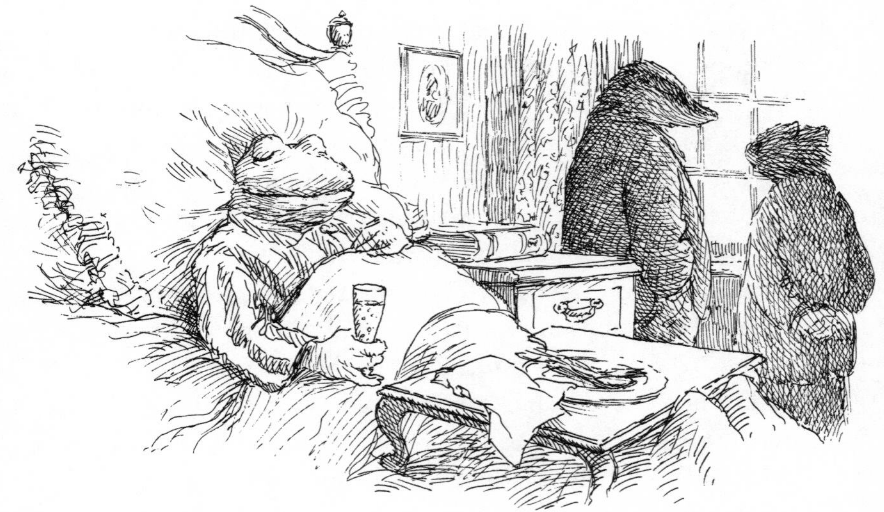

"We must do something about this situation, for it simply cannot be allowed to continue a moment longer!" said the Badger later that day, when Toad had recovered somewhat.

They were in Toad's bedroom, and Toad was now warm and comfortable, his lower half encased by damask sheets and the best lamb's-wool blankets, and his top half propped up by a good many lace-edged pillows, which Miss Bugle had brought in for him.

Spread about the room were the remnants of the luncheon that Mrs Ffleshe's guests had enjoyed more formally in the dining room below. It had been evident even to her that Toad could not be left to recover alone, or his friends left unfed, and so – with some firm prompting from Miss Bugle – trays of food had been brought up, and an enjoyable time had by all.

There had been apologies to Mole, for he had had everything ready for his own party, but though he was grateful for their concern he was, in truth, much happier that Toad was sharing this part of the day with them, albeit in unusual and dramatic circumstances. His own party could wait a day or two longer.

No reference was made by any of them at first to Toad's flight and desperate leap into the River. The circumstances of his doing so had been witnessed and understood by the Mole and the Badger, and the drama had served most of all to underline the extremes to which he had been finally pushed by Mrs Ffleshe.

It was as well that they had been there, as well that they had known how to act, and that the Badger had the firmness to insist on Toad's return to Toad Hall and the privacy of his bedroom. The foolhardiness of Toad's action and the fact that it had endangered the lives of others was not discussed, least of all by Toad himself.

However, lying there at his ease as he now was, the centre of attention, his friends clustered about what might have been his death bed, and clutching a glass of his very best champagne (which, as he explained, was for medicinal rather than celebratory reasons), he had begun to see his action in an heroic light.

"Did I hesitate? I did not! Did I tremble? No! I saw that a bold statement had to be made, and one that she would understand and fear! One of us had to be the first to cast a stone at the Goliath of the River Bank and naturally it had to be myself. Death and oblivion? Did I risk it in the name of our shared liberty? I did. Did I think of myself? I did not. Therefore, my friends, I ask you now to raise your glasses in a toast to one who can fairly claim this day to have fought the good fight and –"

"Toad, I must ask you to desist," growled the Badger. "We are all very glad you survived your own foolishness but the less said on the subject now and in the future the better. Instead, I must ask you as I ask us all to turn our minds to the matter in hand. This annual visitation of Mrs Ffleshe, which has been the ruination of so much, cannot be allowed to continue. To make it plain: we must decide upon a course of action that will rid us of Mrs Ffleshe. I hesitate to say such things about a lady, but then she is no lady who drives her host so far!"

"She *is* a brute," observed the Rat.

"She is worse than a mother-in-law," opined the Otter, who had a distant experience of that particular species of female.

"I confess that she is certainly not someone I would feel especially pleased to welcome to Mole End!" murmured the Mole.

"Well then, what are we to do?" said the Badger.

He stood up and paced about as he often did when he was thinking hard and an idea was imminent. Yet it was the Mole who spoke first.

"I cannot say quite what we should *do*," said he cautiously, "but I would like to make a small suggestion that might lead us to an idea. I believe I am right in saying that the Lord of the Manor in these parts has very considerable jurisdiction in local matters."

"I know all about that," said Toad dismissively, "but unfortunately the gentleman who holds that office is my Uncle Groat, and he's the one who encouraged Nanny Fowle and Mrs Ffleshe to come in the first place."

"Yes, but –" continued the Mole.

"Pooh!" cried Toad. "I hardly think Groat will help us."

"Let us hear Mole out," said the Badger soothingly.

"Unless I am much mistaken, I do not think that anybody in these parts, including you yourself, Toad, has been in touch with Groat in recent years, so we cannot be sure where he stands on these matters. Perhaps if he realised what damage Mrs Ffleshe has done... There can surely be no harm in writing and *telling* him."

"Mmm," said the Badger, nodding his head, "a good point. Well said, Moly!"

"What is more," continued the Mole, who had given considerable thought to the matter since visiting the Village and meeting the Parish Clerk, "might it not be possible to ask Groat to invoke the ancient laws of the Village Court of which he is Lord and Judge and ask him to exile Mrs Ffleshe from the River Bank for ever?"

"You refer to that medieval institution which may in certain circumstances be summoned by the Lord of the Manor, namely Groat?" said the Badger.

"I do!" cried the Mole excitedly, rather relieved that the Badger knew what he was talking about.

"Yes, I have considered that possibility in the past, Mole," said the Badger, "and I believe there is much we could do if Toad's uncle were willing, not least arrest Mrs Ffleshe and clap her in irons –"

"*Arrest* her?" cried Toad excitedly.

"We are talking theoretically, Toad," said the Badger, "so please do not get too excited. Indeed, it is precisely because such notions as these might overexcite your imagination and raise false hopes that I have not mentioned them before.

"The trouble is, Mole," continued the Badger, "in the absence of Groat, nobody else can exercise such jurisdiction and act against her. In fact, she could act against *us* under the ancient laws of vagrant rights, for by virtue of her sojourns at Toad Hall Mrs Ffleshe has earned the right of the Court's protection."

"Do you have any idea what they are talking about, Otter old fellow?" enquired Toad.

"No," replied the Otter truthfully, "no idea at all."

"You, Ratty? Do you understand?"

"I can't say I do," came the response, "but when Badger starts talking like this, and with Mole to give him support, I can't help feeling that something helpful might come out of it."

"Badger," said the Mole, rising and pacing about alongside him, "I confess I didn't quite understand everything I was told by the Parish Clerk, but he did urge me to mention to you his view that after so many years' absence Uncle Groat may be deemed to be – O, drat, I wish I could remember the term he used!"

"*In absentia perpetua*," murmured the Badger, a look of hope coming into his face.

"That's it! In which case, Toad could act in his uncle's place as Lord of the Manor, since *he* is –"

"*De facto* Lord," said the Badger.

"That's right!" exclaimed the Mole. "And – if only he dared – he could –"

"*He* could have Mrs Ffleshe arrested for disturbing the peace!" said the Badger excitedly.

"Could I?" said Toad.

"Or perhaps simply for being a public nuisance," said the Mole.

"Really?" said Toad, sitting up.

"Or for being a nag, and I believe the punishment for that involves the ducking stool!" said the Badger.

"O yes, yes!" cried Toad, rubbing his hands.

"Or, even –" began the Badger, frowning.

"Yes?" asked Toad cheerfully. "What else might I arrest her for, seeing as I am, as I have always believed and as I was born to be, Lord of the Manor and all I can survey from the Village church tower?"

"This is only a technical possibility, Toad, but I suppose you might, if you could prove her guilty of witchcraft, have her burnt at the stake."

"Perhaps that's going a little far," said the Mole, "and I don't think –"

"Well, never mind, never mind – let's get on with it!" said Toad impatiently.

It is often the case that the great tide of history simultaneously sweeps into shore two people with the same idea, each thinking their idea is original. Scientists, inventors, social reformers, even artists and writers rise up and cry "Eureka!" only to hear their cry echoed by another from somewhere across the world

Less usually, however, do those two people have that idea under the same roof, and within the same hour. Yet so it was that Christmas Day at Toad Hall.

While Toad and his friends were beginning to see that a medieval court might be the place to seek just retribution for the sins (if such they were) of Mrs Ffleshe, she and her guests were coming to a similar conclusion regarding Toad.

Mrs Ffleshe had been particularly looking forward to that particular Christmas luncheon, for after many years' trying she had finally won acceptance for her invitation to "The Hall" as she referred to it (she expunged all references to Toad on her invitations) from several personages not only of importance, but of influence as well.

Normally, such people as sons of Law Lords (one of those) brothers of police commissioners (two of those) and widows of bishops (three of those) are cautious about such invitations from those who might be considered parvenus. However, Mrs Ffleshe's decade or more of cultivating these people had finally borne fruit, and all at once. They had all said yes, and they had all been standing on the front steps of the Hall when Toad had gone rushing out.

In addition, and much to Mrs Ffleshe's delight, for it was a most unexpected bonus beyond her wildest dreams, the son of the Law Lord had brought along his father, Lord Mallice, founding partner of the firm Mordant, Mallice and Thrall, a gentleman who more than half the widows and single ladies in the land had been seeking to make the acquaintance of since he had become a widower.

If truth be known, it was the father and not the son Mrs Ffleshe had been interested in and here, the best Christmas present she could have wished for, was his tall, cadaverous, pallid but otherwise delightful form upon her doorstep. She had admired him from afar for many years, following his career to the heights of the legal profession in the columns of *The Times*, and she unashamedly saw in him the final peak in her ascent to the aristocracy.

To win a Lord's hand, what more could an ambitious lady desire?

Imagine her feelings, therefore, when Toad rushed past her as she stepped forward to shake his hand and bowled the object of her desires down the steps and nearly under the wheels of his carriage.

So it was that their luncheon, having been so dramatically blighted by Toad's rushing out, and then by his being carried back in again corpse-like and sopping wet, had got off to a poor start.

It is never easy eating canapés and supping white wine and making polite conversation in such circumstances. Nor when it finally comes – late on this occasion because of the interruptions – does goose look quite so appetising, or stuffing taste quite so delicious, or Brussels sprouts go down quite as easily.

It does not help either when the table has been so carefully laid for nine when only eight sit down, the empty seat being for that gentleman who even now might be taking his last breath in the room above. In such circumstances Christmas toasts and party banter fall flat, very flat indeed.

So it was that for the first hour or so the only sounds to be heard in the dining room of Toad Hall during Mrs Ffleshe's long-planned luncheon were the scraping of cutlery on plates, the clatter of teeth and dentures

chewing at over-roasted parsnips, the clenching of Mrs Ffleshe's jaw and the audible furrowing of her brow.

Yet despite all, and much to her relief, it was Lord Mallice who, as the main course ended, broke the ice by asking his hostess a question that all of them had wished to ask but had dared not.

"This Toad fellah, does he live here?"

"Well, he has… rooms here, yes," said Mrs Ffleshe.

The company relaxed.

"He's a kind of caretaker, then?" pressed Lord Mallice, who in his younger days had built his reputation on the vigour of his cross-examinations. He sensed at once, however, that in Mrs Ffleshe he had finally met a witness who was his match, which perhaps explained the sudden colour in his cheeks and glint in his eye.

"A poor one," said she.

"Would you care to elaborate?"

"We have an important collection of oil paintings here at the Hall and this morning he wantonly destroyed one."

"Dereliction of duty, then?"

"He bruised my arm when I attempted to stop him!"

"Assault and battery."

"And then he encouraged his friends to call me names, terrible names, names such as should never be applied to a lady."

Here, astonishing though it would have seemed to any who had normal dealings with Mrs Ffleshe, she succeeded in squeezing out of her eyes not one but two tears.

"Madam," said Lord Mallice, "take your time, I beg you. Usher, give her a glass of water!" This he addressed to his son, who was well used to his father's forgetting where he was. Indeed, his son had more than once found himself being cross-examined for murder, and at least once for treason, at the breakfast table.

"I ask you now, madam, to tell the court what he encouraged his friends to call you."

There was a hush.

"Brute," she said.

There was a gasp.

"So, to the charges of dereliction of duty and assault and battery must be added libel and slander in the first degree."

"There is more, sir, far more."

"Yes, madam?" said Lord Mallice with relish.

Given this ready opportunity to make an impression,

Mrs Ffleshe took it, and fulsomely. In the space of less than twenty minutes she had set such a catalogue of crimes at Toad's door that Lord Mallice had discovered in them four counts of high treason, in addition to the eight charges of criminal malfeasance, fifteen counts of treacherous negligence and thirty-seven acts of malice aforethought (on which subject his Lordship's reputation had been built).

"In addition," declared Lord Mallice in a smug and satisfied way, "I have lost count of the innumerable lesser charges that arise from the accused's behaviour as an ingrate pernicious, malefactor overt and felon fraudulent, any one of which, in cases where the defendant has a previous conviction, becomes a capital offence. Now then, Mrs Ffleshe, has this gentleman who calls himself Toad of Toad Hall ever, to your knowledge, been convicted of any crime before a court in this land?"

"I believe he has," said Mrs Ffleshe. "He was convicted of stealing motor-cars."

Lord Mallice sighed with pleasure and then raised his arms in a weary way as if to say there was little point in any further questioning.

"It is all up with him," he pronounced solemnly. "I suppose his extraordinary behaviour today could be offered as evidence of an unsound mind in any plea of mitigation, though I believe I might offer a robust defence of the position that he was merely indulging in a foolish act of winter bathing. Then again, the fact is, Mrs Ffleshe, that you have been harbouring a criminal in this house, but I think a sensible judge would not take you to task for that, for you did it from kindly motives, born of pity and ignorance of what he was and is, did you not?"

"I did," said Mrs Ffleshe, attempting to summon up a tear or two more but this time failing. "Out of kindness I did it, and in latter years he has forced me to care for him much against my wishes, and been cruel to me."

"Then I believe we should discuss what we should do over pudding – for I presume that a plum pudding is in the offing, it being Christmas Day. As a Law Lord Emeritus, it is my duty to aid society's victims, of which you are one, so naturally I shall represent you."

It was Mrs Ffleshe's turn to sigh.

"However, as protector of one you now know to be a criminal infernal, if I may use the correct legal phrase, it is *your* duty to turn him over to the law," he continued. "We have present here two gentlemen related to the fraternity of police commissioners who can be sworn in at once and can arrest him. We also have at least one lady, so far silent, who is I believe a bishop's wife, and maybe more, whose moral views can therefore be taken as unimpeachable, though it might be prudent at this juncture to ascertain what they are."

Lord Mallice turned to the youngest of the bishops' widows.

"Madam," said he, "how do you think we should act in the best interest of the soul of this soul-less defendant?"

"What I have heard of him is quite scandalous!" cried the bishop's widow. "And I believe he should be given a fair trial and condemned, and as soon as possible."

By now the mood of the luncheon party had changed for the better, for there is nothing more enjoyable in a group of people than to find a common enemy.

A lively discussion ensued as the plum pudding was served, and then brandies and cigars – a discussion at which, though in normal circumstances they would have retired that the men might smoke, the ladies were invited to stay, and contribute, which all did forcibly.

"To sum up," said Lord Mallice later, "the verdict of this jury is that he is guilty till proved even more guilty and that it would be a pity if his case were to be allowed to clog up the courts for years, during which time he would continue to live at the cost of the taxpayer. We therefore seek justice that is fair but swift and summary, and in that matter I have a suggestion to make."

"Please, My Lord," said Mrs Ffleshe, whose delight at having Lord Mallice to lunch had developed first into pleasure and then adoration, an emotion he appeared to return, "will you accept some more brandy before you make that suggestion?"

"From your fair hand, madam, I would accept a glass of water and believe it to be brandy," said he gallantly, for rarely had he found so eloquent and satisfactory a witness as his hostess.

"O My Lord!" she sighed. "This truly is a Happy Christmas."

"So," said Lord Mallice, gathering his wits once more, "I believe there are grounds to arrest this gentleman at once and have him in court on the morrow, and swinging on the gallows the day following, if such is to be his punishment, in time for us all to return to tea and scones, even allowing for his appeal, which will be dismissed on my personal recommendation.

“I am certain this can be achieved because I took the liberty on my way here today of calling in at the Village to affirm a curious historic fact of which I had read, namely, that no Act of Parliament was ever passed repealing the rights of the Lordship of this parish to try its own cases, and mete out its own justice.

“Indeed, there still remains a working gaol where the criminal can be safely held, a court house where he can be fairly tried, a dungeon that holds implements of persuasion which may be reasonably used to extract the truth and thus save much time in cross-examination, and a method of punishment that is as final as they come, namely hanging, drawing and quartering.

“Around this very table we have all the officials we need to arrest the suspect, stand witness to his crimes, act as prosecutor and judge and finally, if one of the widows of the late bishops here will agree, to offer spiritual support to the accused, hear his confession and administer last rites.

"To complete matters, and make them entirely legal, we have a Parish Clerk in the Village who has satisfied me that he is ready, eager and able to make the correct entries in the trial, punishment and mortality rolls – though my conversation with him earlier today was purely hypothetical. I little imagined that I would encounter such a hardened criminal upon whom I might try out this local justice. I have rarely met a Clerk so very eager to do this work and if he is willing to do it over the Christmas recess then I have little doubt that I can secure for him a knighthood.

"Now, may I suggest we toast our good fortune that the spirit of Christmas should have put so interesting and wholesome a case our way? After that we must act quickly and arrest the criminal Toad."

"Sir," said Mrs Ffleshe, "I should warn you that he has a gang of low-class fellows in his employ of whom we should be wary – a threat to their leader might lead them to extreme actions."

"Who are they?" said Mallice in a grim voice.

"The first, and strongest, is Badger, an idle woodsman. His friend is a water rat known locally as Ratty – he is a waterman of the cunning sort and not to be trusted. Otter is an idle fellow with a son who to my knowledge has no mother, so you can imagine what class of person he is. O yes, sir! That is the low sort they are! And, finally, there is one who calls himself Mr Mole of Mole

End. He puts on a respectable front, which causes me to think he may be more dangerous and corrupt than the rest of them put together!"

"Then we need reinforcements before we attempt to make an arrest," said Lord Mallice. "Can we summon some help from the Village perhaps?"

"I can do better than that," said Mrs Ffleshe.

"Madam, you are a woman of infinite resource," cried Lord Mallice with passion, involuntarily taking her hand in his own.

"The Villagers are a knock-kneed lot," said she, entwining her fingers in his. "However, those who live in the Wild Wood, namely the weasels and stoats, have been harshly treated by Toad's gang in the recent past, from what I hear. I shall send a message out to them and I believe we shall soon have all the help we need."

"Let it be so!" said Lord Mallice delightedly, most reluctantly releasing her hand. "Let it be so!"

Toad and his friends had debated the question of arresting Mrs Ffleshe long and hard, and all but the Mole preferred this course of action. For though the impetus for that idea had come from him, he had had second thoughts, pointing out that Christmas Day was a time for peace, charity and goodwill and perhaps if they all spoke to Mrs Ffleshe nicely...

The others, particularly the practical Water Rat, were unconvinced.

"Give such an enemy half a chance and they attack first, eh Otter?"

Otter nodded.

"Well, at least we could go to the Village and talk to the Parish Clerk again," said the Mole.

"We might," said the Badger, who was standing by the window, "but see how the day is already growing dark and if I am not mistaken a great deal colder – and – good heavens!"

His sudden alarm brought silence, and his whispered command to blow out the candles was instantly obeyed.

"What is it, Badger?"

"Look! There, in the shadows. *There!*"

They looked and saw: weasels and stoats, a good many of them.

"And over there! I can scarcely believe it!"

Making his way to the Hall's front door, bold as brass, was the Chief Weasel, an unpleasant character known to them all, and at his side several hench-stoats.

No sooner did he knock at the front door than Toad's bedroom door opened and in hurried Miss Bugle in some distress.

"Mr Toad, sir, it's the weasels and stoats. They've surrounded the house and now the gentlemen who came to luncheon are coming up the stairs with a warrant for your arrest. Fly, sir, fly!"

"Badger and I will delay 'em," cried the Rat even as they heard the sounds of heavy, determined footsteps on the main stairs. "Otter and Mole, you'd better get Toad out of the Hall to safety as fast as you can!"

"But – but I'm still in my nightshirt," spluttered Toad, "and I haven't finished my champagne –"

"No time for that!" said the Mole with determination, grabbing his dressing gown and hurrying him to the bedroom door. "Miss Bugle, lead the way!"

It was not a moment to argue, or dawdle. As the Rat and the Badger took up their stations at the top of the stairs to confront the arresting officers, Mole and Toad followed Miss Bugle to the back stairs, with the Otter taking up their rear.

What instinct was it that told the fugitives that a posse of weasels and stoats awaited them on the cobbles outside the kitchen door? Whatever its name, it prompted them to change their plans swiftly. They stopped short of opening the door, and Toad and Mole crept inside the coal cellar – which Mole knew all too well – and allowed Miss Bugle to shut and bolt the door upon them.

While Otter and Miss Bugle hurried back to help Rat and Badger, Mole and Toad stood in silence, with lumps of anthracite in their hands as weapons in case they had to make a fight of it, as they listened to the search parties running back and forth above their heads, and up and down the Hall stairs.

They were not discovered, and when dusk fell outside they did not wait for Miss Bugle to risk her own safety by releasing them, but put into operation a plan that the Mole had considered when he had been confined in this same place, but which he could not act upon for lack of a helper.

"Toad," he commanded firmly, for Toad was shivering with fear as well as cold, "kneel down so that I can climb on to your back."

In other circumstances he would have done this service for Toad, and let his host raise the coal-hole cover and climb out first, but the sad truth was that he did not trust him. He rather fancied that once Toad sniffed the freedom of the fresh air above he would do a bunk and leave Mole behind, just as he had before.

Toad whinged and whined but the Mole would have none of it.

"Kneel down, Toad," he whispered urgently, "or I shall call for help and turn you over to the law!"

This did the trick, and soon the Mole was on Toad's back, pushing at the heavy cover above his head before finally pulling himself to freedom.

There were some horse harnesses hanging from a nail nearby and these he attached to a post and dropped down to Toad so that he could clamber up. Then they scampered across the drive and crept beneath a hedge till it got dark, shaking and shivering with cold.

Several times patrols of weasels and stoats went by, and once a brace of policemen. Then, when the coast seemed clear, they crawled right under the hedge, across the lane, into the field beyond and crept by starlight down towards the River.

Their plan was to make their way to the bridge and, if they could cross it undetected, to try to reach the safety of Otter's house, for they were sure that a search party would have been sent to Mole End.

That the Mole should thus find himself a fugitive from the law with Toad was not, in truth, something he had expected upon Christmas Day. Yet, he reflected, since that fateful first meeting with Ratty two years before, he had found himself in a great many situations that his humdrum life till then could not have led him to expect. He trusted he might in time look back on this particular adventure with a degree of equanimity, but for the moment –

"*What's that?*"

Toad suddenly clutched his arm, indicating that he had heard something coming through the reeds towards them.

"It's nothing, Toad, please keep calm," said the Mole in a mollifying way. "Now, we had better –"

"And *that*?"

Toad clutched his arm again and it was all Mole could do to keep him still and low.

"Really, Toad, it is nothing but your imagination. Now follow me and we'll be at the bridge in no time. Our pursuers have probably long since given up the chase."

Mole's voice slowed, for this time it was he who thought he had heard something, and seen something as well. It was a low whistle he heard, and sudden lights he saw, red lights, but strangely fierce, as of some ferocious night creature on the far bank.

"Come on, Toad, there's nothing there," said Mole bravely.

O, but there was. All about them in the dark they heard sinister sliding and slurrying, strange warning grunts and half-screams, malicious clicks and knocks, and caught brief glimpses of livid eyes, and shining teeth and weapons catching the dim night light.

"O, Mole," said Toad in a terrified voice, "they're after us! Better to be caught at once than have to bear this ghastly suspense."

"Pull yourself together," said the Mole firmly, though he greatly regretted he had not thought to bring along a few lumps of coal to serve as weapons. "We'll soon be at the bridge."

He was right. Its arch loomed in the darkness ahead of them and seemed quite deserted.

"Listen, Toad," said the Mole. "Please try to stop your teeth chattering and your knees knocking, and keep your eyes cast down, for I can see their whites quite clearly in the dark."

"O Moly," moaned Toad, "we are done for. They will stalk us through the night and roast us alive on their spits for their Christmas feast."

"When I say 'go!', we shall go," said Mole. "Keep in the shadow of the bridge wall and do not make a sound. *Do you understand?*"

"Don't you think we should just give ourselves up?" said Toad in a thin, quavering voice. "Then perhaps they will show mercy and put us to death at once – O! *O! O!*"

These exclamations of alarm followed the sudden drumming of feet beneath the bridge, and then a high, cackling laugh.

"We can see you, Toad, we can see you!"

"O Mole," said Toad, "I can't bear it!"

With that, Toad broke free of Mole and the shadows in which they hid, and ran out on to the road, his hands raised in the air. "I am here! Torment me no more! Take me!"

It did occur to Mole that this offered himself the perfect opportunity of escape, but he could not bring himself to do it. He ran after Toad, caught up with him, and stood protectively at his side as from the shadows of the ditches on either side of the bridge stoats and weasels emerged, grinning, cackling and whetting their weapons for what seemed likely to be the kill.

But as Toad fainted clean away, and Mole stood firm to fight what he felt sure was his last fight, some larger figures loomed out of the night – lords and ladies, and several constables, and in no time at all the two fugitives were put in handcuffs.

Soon the Mole was on Toad's back, pushing at the heavy cover... *(p. 155)*

They were led back to Toad Hall, on whose steps Mrs Ffleshe waited with a rolling pin.

"That's him," she cried, pointing at Toad, "and that's the villainous Mr Mole of Mole End."

The game was up, it seemed. The only comfort that the Mole found in this situation was that in the chaos and gloom he noticed the Otter making his escape in one direction while Miss Bugle went off in another. Where they went to the Mole did not see, but he hoped they might perhaps make a rendezvous with the Badger and the Rat at some later time.

In this the Mole judged his friends well, for those two sterling animals had done their best to halt the advance of Mrs Ffleshe's allies, and confuse the chase. Now they appeared to protest Toad and Mole's innocence, but were warned that they might be arrested for obstructing the police. They were escorted to the boundary of Toad's estate and told to go peaceably home. They did not, however. Instead, they watched from beyond the line of weasels and stoats who stood as gloating guards at the gates, and from this frustrating situation witnessed the final humiliation of Toad and Mole.

For Lord Mallice appeared on the steps of the Hall next to Mrs Ffleshe, and by candlelight he read out three token charges against the manacled Toad: for treason, for murderous assault and for failing to declare himself a criminal. While against the handcuffed Mole was laid the charge of resisting arrest.

He then gave orders for the criminals to be conveyed post-haste to the Village Gaol, there to await the pleasure of the Lord of the Manor, or his representative.

Toad and Mole were roughly taken to Lord Mallice's carriage and handcuffed to its rear like common criminals on the way to the gallows. In vain did Toad protest. It mattered not that he was master of the Hall and they his guests, and the weasels and stoats all trespassers.

With the crack of a whip the carriage set off and Toad's cries and shouts were drowned out by the sonorous noise of the carriage wheels as they turned across his cobbles.

"An 'appy exmas, Mr Toad!" mocked the weasels.

"And a hespecially Merry Christmas to you, sir, Mr Mole!" laughed the stoats, who were only too happy to gain their revenge upon an animal who had fought and beaten them on that historic occasion a year or two before when they had been ousted after their illegal takeover of Toad Hall.

"Fiends," growled the Badger as his two friends were dragged by, forced to run to keep up with the carriage and prevent themselves falling on their faces in the mud and dirt.

"We'll think of something, Mole!" called out the Rat. "Toad, keep your spirits up, we'll get justice for you!"

· IX ·
Under Lock and Key

By the time they reached the Village the two accused were exhausted from the struggle of keeping up with the coach to which they had been so cruelly tied. They were so enfeebled that neither was capable of offering any resistance at their moment of final confinement.

The Parish Clerk, having been forewarned by a horseback rider that criminals had been arrested in the Parish and were being sent to him "at the behest of the *de facto* representative of the Lord of Session and of the Manor", did not hesitate to do his duty and abandon his Christmas fireside. Indeed, he was delighted to do so, for the case sounded like a capital one and would mean he could end his days as Parish Clerk on a high note.

For this reason the fact that it was Mr Toad of Toad Hall who was the main accused, and Mr Mole of Mole End who was his accomplice, and that he had a high regard for both, mattered not to the Parish Clerk. In any case the cast-iron wheels of justice had begun to turn, and it was his ancient duty and bounden task to oil them, and see they continued to turn as smoothly as they might.

He was therefore ready and waiting on the bridge when they arrived, a great ring of keys in his hand, the padlocks of the Gaol already undone and its door invitingly left open at the bottom of the steps which the Mole had descended with such curiosity only two days before.

Now, with the roar of the river in their ears, and the clanking of their handcuffs, they were led down the steps and into the gloom of the Gaol by the Clerk, who carried a storm lantern to light the way.

"You will find every comfort within," said he in a friendly way, "as is prescribed by ancient statute. There is a stone slab for your bed, which will accommodate you both, a bucket for water from the culvert, and your food will be passed through this flap in the door once a day. In addition, there is a window to give you light, and a grille in the door which will do likewise. A candle has been lit to give you even more light and warmth. Guard it well, for it is the only one you will have this week."

"Is there no food?" cried Toad pitiably.

"You have missed your meal today, gentlemen, but fear

not, a dry crust of bread will be served in the morning."

Toad groaned, while the Mole attempted a feeble protest till the Clerk interrupted him.

"Be of good cheer, for you are fortunate indeed to have been arraigned in the festive season, when I am glad to say that the rules permit your gaoler (which is to say myself) a degree of latitude!"

A look of hope came to Toad's eye, and visions of good food of the kind so essential for his daily comfort.

"Now, I would normally be permitted in these circumstance to allow you a roast goose or two, cranberry and apple sauces, and plenty of choice roasted vegetables, but –"

"But what?" cried Toad.

"But since you have a previous conviction, Mr Toad, and the current charges are so very serious, my generosity must be statutorily restrained to the provision of a mite of beef dripping each."

"A mite?" said Toad. "How much is that?"

"Two mites make a snip, which is less than a peck but rather more than a pinch!"

With this the two felons were thrust into the Gaol and the door locked for the night.

Mole, having already examined the Gaol from the outside, had very little doubt that getting out again was not going to be easy. Nevertheless, he set about examining the place to see what possible avenues of escape it offered. He also thought that it would be prudent if he and Toad were to empty their pockets to see what articles they had that might help them either escape or be more comfortable.

Toad proved less resourceful. The moment the door slammed shut upon them, he slumped down on the slab and put his head in his hands.

"We are done for, Mole, if they leave us here overnight. Look! It is so cold that the water in this bucket has frozen!"

He suddenly rose up in a panic and, grasping the bars of the door, cried, "Help! Help! A gold guinea to anyone who helps us escape!"

The Parish Clerk peered in. "This is my first and final warning, Mr Toad. Any further attempts to bribe the gaoler will result in your trial by ordeal taking place sooner and not later, as decreed by Act of Parliament."

"What trial by ordeal?" stammered Toad.

"Which is to say whose trial or what ordeal?" asked the Clerk.

"Well, both I suppose," said Toad.

"Your trial, sir, and Mr Mole's. As for the ordeals, their nature, number and order will be read out to you prior to their execution by the Clerk to the Parish, which is myself, but you will find comfort in the fact that following the Act of Repeal of 1244 there are only twelve trials, beginning with the rack and ending, as is customary in most countries in the civilised world, with the fiery stake.

"Now, if you will forgive me, I must retire and make ready the instruments and utensils we shall be needing, for some of them are a little blunt and rusty, and I believe that we may have difficulty with the ratchet on the rack as my stores are quite out of pig's blubber. As for the wheel of fortune I fear that it turns rather too clumsily (which is to say that even in the hands of an expert, which I am not, it is wont to tear its victims apart rather than simply stretch them) and I really must try to see to it, if I have time. So I bid you good night, sirs, with compliments of the season."

"Tear us apart? Fiery stake? The rack? O Mole, this will be the end of me! Save me, Moly, and Toad Hall will be yours! I would rather live in your humble abode for the rest of my life than be put to these torments!"

"My humble abode is very comfortable, thank you very much, Toad," said the Mole a little tartly. "So now let us examine our situation more calmly, starting with these items here."

Between them they had some lucifers, a red spotted handkerchief, a cigar, and a florin (Toad's), and a fruit knife, safety pin, white handkerchief, paper and pencil (Mole's).

"Now listen, Toad, I think we should ask ourselves what Ratty would do with these objects if he were a prisoner in our stead, for he is a master of making-do."

No sound came from Toad but the chattering of teeth, though whether from the freezing cold or abject fear the Mole was in no mood to enquire.

"Well then," said he as cheerfully as he could and realising he must take charge once more, "I think Ratty would advise us to sit upon our handkerchiefs to keep ourselves as warm as possible. Then he would tell us to blow out this candle and conserve it. It will be a source of heat and warmth later tonight, and perhaps, if occasion arises, we can use it as a signal to our rescuers."

"As you wish," said Toad apathetically.

"But before I blow it out, let us see if there is any possible escape," continued the Mole.

The candle allowed him to examine their cell a little more, showing that the only places of egress apart from the heavily padlocked door were the barred window and the culvert in one corner, which evidently went down into the river below, and now roared and gurgled in a threatening way.

"With the help of the bucket and rope," said the Mole, "this offers us a source of water, but I very much doubt that it would be a safe way to escape. However, Ratty is the most practical animal alive and I am sure he will find a way to get us out of here, or help us escape when we are conveyed to the Court House. And you may be sure that Badger and Otter will help as well."

Toad remained silent for a long time, till at last he said rather miserably, "And Miss Bugle, I'm sure she will help if Mrs Ffleshe allows it, for she has always helped get me out of scrapes before. Don't you think?"

"I do, old fellow," said the Mole comfortingly. "Now, since it is Christmas night why don't we cheer ourselves up a little by remembering better and happier nights than this one?"

"You begin, Mole, for I don't think I have the strength to talk."

"Well then," said the Mole, blowing out the candle and taking up his place beside Toad, "did I ever tell you about – about – I –"

For a moment their plight, his tiredness, and disappointment that the day had gone so terribly wrong, got the better of the Mole. His voice trembled and he was close to tears.

Then he felt Toad's arms about his shoulders, and heard Toad say, "Mole, old chap, we're in a sorry mess, but I've faced worse, and will face worse still in the future. Meanwhile, there's no animal I'd rather be locked up with than yourself, for you never fail to cheer me up and you only rarely admonish me. Now, what were you going to tell me?"

The Mole was greatly touched by Toad's unexpected words and he reflected that, exasperating though he could sometimes be, when all was said and done, his heart was in the right place.

"Ah yes, Toad. I was going to tell you about a Christmas night that happened long before I left my home and came to Mole End. It concerns how I was rescued from a most dangerous situation by my sister, whom I don't believe..."

"No, you've not mentioned any sister that I recall."

"My, but it was a bitter night – a good deal colder than this one! – and the river we lived by was certainly in much worse condition than the one that races by these walls at this very moment. Foolishly, and against all advice, I had set forth into the night to take a relative some mince pies, when..."

The faith that Toad and Mole put in their friends was well placed, and already amply justified.

Some time after they had been dragged through the gates of Toad Hall behind the carriage of Lord Mallice and off towards the Village, the Otter appeared at Badger and Ratty's side, breathless and muddy. He had made good his escape through the gardens of Toad Hall, and decided it would be more prudent to lie low till the coast was clear.

"But what of Miss Bugle?" asked the Badger, very much concerned for Toad's loyal housekeeper whom neither he nor the Rat had seen since the fracas.

"She is down by the boathouse recovering from her ordeal, but quite determined never to go back to Toad

Hall till Mrs Ffleshe departs the place for ever. She is anxious to see you, Badger, for she has information which may be pertinent to Toad's situation."

The animals laid low a little longer, for there were patrols of weasels and stoats about, but finally, as night deepened and the temperature dropped towards freezing, their taste for patrolling rapidly waned. One by one, group by group, they deserted their posts and sneaked back to Toad Hall and the comfort of kitchen warmth and sustenance, from where their ribald, triumphant laughter issued forth.

Badger and the others made haste to the boathouse and there found the inestimable Miss Bugle awaiting them. That retiring middle-aged spinster whom the Mole had got to know so well over the last few days was now utterly transformed.

By the light of the candles that she had somehow contrived to bring with her – as well as sufficient sustenance for each of them and a parcel of clothes for Toad – they saw that there was new colour in her cheeks and vivacity in her eyes, and it was clear that the day's extraordinary events had affected her deeply.

"Not only must we do something, gentlemen," said she, "but we *shall* do something!"

Badger nodded approvingly and observed, "It would help us greatly if you could give us any intelligence you may have regarding the intentions of the tyrants now in residence in the Hall."

"That I can, sir," she said. "When I realised the direction in which their luncheon conversation was going I broke a rule of a lifetime and took the liberty of listening to all I could from behind the door. Their intentions are far more dastardly than I would ever have suspected possible."

Quickly she told them of Lord Mallice's advice that medieval laws should be invoked to punish Toad, and now presumably the Mole as well; and of much else besides.

"I believe there is only one sure way of getting Toad released before the worst rigours of brutal medieval law are applied to him," said the Badger, "and that is to prevail upon his Uncle Groat, who is the true Lord of the Manor, to come to his aid."

"But he lives in a northern county," said the Rat, "which is surely too far away for us to get word to him quickly, even if he were willing to be persuaded by a mere letter or telegraph."

"That is all true," said the Badger, "but we should remember the words Mole admonished us with but two evenings ago – where there's a will there's a way. Let us prove him right. The only way of getting Groat to act and save his nephew is to see him personally. Nothing is so persuasive. Now, the only two people here who have met him, and know his history intimately, as well as the full story of Mrs Ffleshe's coming to the Hall and its consequences, are myself and you, Miss Bugle.

"I will not prevaricate, madam. I believe it is essential that we set forth immediately to that northern county where Groat now lives and beard the lion in his den."

"Sir," cried Miss Bugle passionately, "if you had not suggested it I would have done so myself! Nothing will stop me from going to see him now to prevent what seems otherwise certain to be a grave miscarriage of justice against my master. But my passage north, be it by night and day and through the blizzard snows of winter, will no doubt be safer and more swift if I journey under your protection!"

"The swiftest way north is by the Lathbury Road," said the Rat, "and if I am not mistaken Mole told us that Mr Baltry the poulterer had reason to dislike Mrs Ffleshe. Perhaps with the help of his conveyance he can transport Badger and Miss Bugle to a railway station."

These plans were soon agreed, and it remained only for the Rat and the Otter to undertake to journey at once to the Village, and see what help they might be able to offer Toad and Mole.

"It will be better if we take my boat and go by way of the canal, and that tributary that will take us covertly to the Village. If only we can get them out of gaol and evade further capture till Badger and Miss Bugle return with a pardon we may have a chance of saving our friends. If that venture fails then we may at least have time to gain some local support for Toad and perhaps bring about his escape by force. The weasels and stoats are poor fighters when it comes to it!"

"So be it," said the Badger, rising and blowing out the candles. "We shall not make the mistake of going back to our homes for provisions, for the weasels and stoats may be lying in wait for us – always assuming they have the stomach for such action on so cold a night, which I very much doubt. If you are willing, Miss Bugle, we shall begin our long journey right away."

"I am!" said that brave lady.

Out into the cold night air they went, making their way first to the Iron Bridge where one lone guard remained. The Otter quickly overcame him and tied him up, then Badger and Miss Bugle, with a brief word of farewell to the others, crossed over the raging River and turned north for Lathbury.

When their friends were safely out of sight, the Rat and the Otter untied the hapless guard, so that he wouldn't freeze solid in the night, and sent him packing to the Wild Wood with dire warnings of what they would do to him if they met him again this side of Twelfth Night.

Then they made their way to the Rat's boat, which was moored nearby in the safer waters of the canal, and began their surreptitious journey towards the Village.

* * *

"Toad?" whispered the Mole some time in the night.

But Toad was asleep and happily oblivious of their situation. He had pulled his dressing gown about him, and now leaned against the wall, breathing restlessly.

They had spoken of many things, but most of all of Christmas past, of Toad Senior, his generosity and his passing this very night so many years before; and of the Mole's sister, and her expertise at making homes and their occupants feel well blessed, and how sad it was that time and distance had lost her.

He rose stiffly and climbing up on to the slab reached up to the window above. Holding on to its bars, he could just glimpse the night sky, and the shift of cloud made lurid by a moon that had begun to rise.

"My goodness!" he exclaimed with pleasure. For as his eyes adjusted to the night outside he saw that it had begun to snow, and heavily.

He climbed down from their stony bed and felt his way to the door. Through the bars, in the light of the moon, he could see the snow beginning to settle on the steps outside.

The church clock chimed – one, two, three, four.

"Four o'clock," whispered the Mole.

He felt cold through and through, and yet not so in his heart and spirit. Why, there had been much in his conversation with Toad that had inspired and cheered him, and Toad as well he fancied. Indeed, he could not remember so enjoyable a Christmas night conversation as this for very many years! In fact, not since that night when his sister had –

"I am being foolish," the Mole told himself, "and

perhaps light-headed, for our position is truly a parlous one, and yet – and yet – did my sister not always say that a fall of snow before the dawn of Boxing Day was a mark of good fortune, for it counted as a white Christmas? I believe she did! No wonder I feel so sure we shall be rescued!"

The snow swirled in the moonlight, thickened, parted, turned and raced.

"O, it *will* be a merry Christmas," the Mole told himself, "just as it once used to be. I'm sure of it!"

·X·
Rescue

Toad and Mole's hopes for an early release from their cruel confinement were dashed on Boxing Day, when nobody visited them at all. Then, when nobody came on the day following, and *again* on the day following that, even the optimistic Mole began to feel low.

Their cell was bitterly cold, and though the water in the culvert had not frozen, any they left in the bottom of their bucket froze solid in minutes. To add to their distress, the raging roar of the river seemed to be growing ever louder and more rapacious, and its thundering wearied them.

Their only comfort was the crust of bread and beef dripping that the Parish Clerk pushed through the flap in their door each morning and then, on the third morning, a blanket each, together with the parcel containing Toad's clothes, sent by Miss Bugle and delivered to the Parish Clerk by Mr Baltry.

Yet, despite these difficulties, the prisoners were astonished to find that with each day that passed their ability to endure the cold and discomforts of their cell increased, as did their pleasure in what little food they had.

This owed much to the resourceful Mole, who had the very good idea of throwing a few crumbs of their bread into the bottom of the culvert to attract any small fry that might live there. Having earlier submerged the bucket in the water it needed only a deft flick of his wrist at Mole's command for Toad to haul aloft a bucketful of stickleback and one or two crayfish.

Mole thought that by combining this small catch with a few dried leaves of wild mint that had made its home that summer on the windowsill above their heads, along with the beef dripping, he might make something palatable. He heated it all up in the bottom of the metal bucket by means of the candle, and after some experimentation created a dish to rival his well-known Stickleback Pie.

"It's certainly original," said Mole, licking his lips.

"Original, Moly? It's a work of brilliance that would grace the table of my club in Town!" said Toad, glad that something was finally going their way. "The addition of the crayfish juice just as you serve it is a stroke of genius. If we put it in little jars and gave it a name such as

'Prisoner's Relish' I believe we could sell it throughout the Empire for at least a penny three farthings a time.

"Of course, the fact that I am so well known and admired is not something we should forget. If we were to add an image of my head on the label (for which I would charge you only a nominal fee) and declared that it was manufactured in the 'Famous Kitchens of Toad Hall' and had been eaten by the monarchs of Europe, I believe you would very soon be somewhat better off, whilst I would become very wealthy indeed!"

But such interludes could not hide the fact that both animals were beginning to weaken under the stress of their situation, which was not helped by not knowing when their trial would be held. So it was with great relief that their cell door was opened on the morning of New Year's Eve and the Parish Clerk entered in.

"Gentlemen," said he, "I am very glad you are still alive for I thought you might have suffered from the cold (which is to say become frozen, solid). I imagine you wish to know when you are to be tried and executed? That information I cannot impart."

He talked at length in this ambiguous manner and eventually the two animals became too hungry and cold to understand all that he said. However, he did let slip the information that the main cause of the delay was that "the bad weather has made it difficult for the specialist craftsmen who are needed to prepare the Court for the trial (by which I mean your ordeal) to travel to the Village and ply their skills."

Toad did not like the sound of "specialist craftsmen" and asked for clarification on the matter.

"There has been a good deal of interest in your case amongst the legal profession and gentlemen of the press, who together have suggested that it is essential that matters are seen to be conducted fairly, according to the proper rules and regulations that govern trials by ordeal.

"In the interests of justice and fair play these kind-hearted gentlemen have been generous enough to provide sufficient funds for me to be able to hire the mangle-makers, tong tuners, corkscrew turners, and tine sharpeners who can modernise our antiquated instruments of trial."

"That *is* kind of them," said Toad.

"It is, sir," said the Parish Clerk, "and very gratifying, too. In consequence, and at their request, I have increased the seating capacity at the Court House. Tickets are being issued for the event starting at one shilling for those who will be outside and there able to see you dragged into Court, to the most expensive – and these are already sold out – being ten guineas for a seat adjacent to the Royal Box. That construction, incidentally, is likely to be occupied by His Royal Highness the Prince himself, and those members of the Royal Hunt who have expressed a wish to be in at the kill (which is to say execution of sentence)."

"But surely the Court House is large enough already without adding more seats?" said Mole, remembering the huge chamber.

"Not nearly capacious enough for the multitudes who are showing such patriotic interest in justice, and such very great social concern for – and scholarly interest in – the medieval practice of the law. You see, gentlemen, our

Village's Court Baron, which is presided over by the Lord of Session or his representative, remains the sole exemplar of its type extant and in working order.

"It is now being very widely suggested that if your case is successful (by which I mean if you are found guilty and satisfactorily punished) then the law of the land, which has erred too long on the side of mercy and the offender, will be changed back to what it was several hundred years ago. That will be a happy day for us all, will it not?"

"But when *will* we be tried?" enquired the Mole.

"No later than New Year a twelve-month or two," said the Parish Clerk, "which is to say within three years."

"Three years!" cried Toad when the Parish Clerk was gone. "By then I shall be but a shadow of my former self, assuming I am alive at all."

"Calm yourself, Toad," interjected Mole; "our friends know our plight and will soon be here to rescue us!"

"You said that yesterday and the day before, and the day before that!" responded Toad. "And still they do not come. I am in despair, Mole! I cannot go on much longer! To think that Ratty and Otter saved me after I plunged into the River only to abandon me here. I wish I had perished then!"

"But, Toad, just think of how many you will disappoint if you do not stand trial. Why, it seems that the whole county will be watching, and many in the Town."

"The county, the Town – watching *me*?"

"I am sure of it," said the Mole.

"Just one county, just one Town, or do you think other counties and other Towns – perhaps the whole land?"

"More than likely," said the Mole. "The gentlemen of the press will be very eager to hear you speak in your own defence."

"Goodness," cried Toad, "I had not thought of that! You are right – I must begin to practise my speeches at once so that I do not disappoint my public. Naturally I shall be making several speeches."

"Several?"

"Of course. First for my plea, which will seek to demonstrate the passion with which I believe in my own innocence! Then for my defence, to show how mistaken are these charges! Next my speech before my ordeal, which will move many to tears! After that will be my various speeches upon the rack, hanging in chains, in the mangle, caught amidst the tines, and I shall entertain the masses with my eloquence even as I burn at the fiery stake!"

"Do you think that you will be in any fit condition to make speeches at such moments?" enquired the Mole, who was not at all certain on the point and was growing increasingly concerned that he too might have to make a speech.

"Of course, Mole, of course. Creating speeches is to me what creating a new relish is to you. But fear not: I am an expert at such things. I will even rehearse you in your lines so that you don't let me down."

"That is most kind of you, Toad, and since we cannot be sure when we will go on trial I suggest you begin your preparation at once."

Toad immediately began to pace about the little cell proclaiming his innocence with lofty words and sentiments, and in particular practising his openings and endings, for it was his considered opinion that it was upon those that the success of a speech most often depended.

By such means the thoughtful Mole managed to keep Toad preoccupied and to divert him from those moments of dark gloom that were prone to overtake him. His own fears he kept to himself, along with his occasional doubts that they would ever be rescued. But these never lasted long, for he knew that if there were any animals in the wide world who could be trusted to come to their aid it was their River Bank friends.

By midnight on New Year's Eve Toad was already asleep, exhausted from a day of speechifying, but the Mole was still awake. He stood, as he did every night, at the grille in the Gaol door, staring at the night sky as the nearby church clock heralded the arrival of the New Year. Since he was in the habit of making resolutions, he made one now: "If ever – no! *when* – I am set free, the first thing I shall do when the weather gets better is to journey north and meet my sister once again!"

Mole's trust in their friends was well justified, for while the Badger and Miss Bugle travelled north in pursuit of Toad's Uncle Groat, the Rat and the Otter had by no means been idle.

The initial idea of a direct approach to the Village Gaol had been thwarted by the stoats and weasels, who had taken up positions around the Village, and particularly in the vicinity of the Gaol itself.

The Parish Clerk had provided the Wild Wooders with food and warmth – the latter in the form of braziers which burned brightly in the High Street and along the bridge and greatly increased the guards' morale. As for food, this was freely supplied from the well-stocked larders of Toad Hall, and Toad would not have been pleased to know that he was footing the bill of victualling the very forces deputed to watch over him. Naturally enough, the offer of second helpings to those who undertook guarding duties ensured plenty of recruits for that tedious and chilly task.

This initial setback did not put off the Rat and the Otter for long. Two nights later they succeeded in penetrating the Village's lines by boat, and under cover of darkness they were able to examine the Gaol from the outside. They very rapidly concluded that an assault upon it would probably end in their own arrest.

"The door is too well padlocked and the walls too thick for direct assault," the Rat whispered.

"And that window's too high and narrow for easy access, even if we could furnish Toad and Mole with tools to loosen the bars," concluded the Otter.

To make matters worse they failed utterly in their attempts to attract their friends' attention because the roar of the river's flow was so great that their surreptitious cries could not be heard, and they dared not risk alerting the stoat who stood guard near the door itself. Even so, they were heard and then seen by some of the other guards, and had to beat a hasty retreat.

In addition to these difficulties, the Rat had quickly established that all their homes, including Mole End, were being spied on by the Wild Wooders for signs of activity.

"So even if we got them out, Otter, what would we do with them? Since it seems that the trial will not take place for a few days yet, we have time to prepare a bolt-hole. I suggest that Toad's boathouse would be the safest place to hide – it is accessible by water, yet nearly impossible to raid from that direction, and it would be very hard for our enemies to flush us out before we made good our escape, which might be in one of several directions.

"I therefore think we should return to our respective homes and appear to live normal lives by day, whilst working at night to ready the boathouse for our friends' escape. The weather is so bitter that the Wild Wooders' vigilance is bound to decline when night falls, so we can make our move then."

"Meanwhile," observed the Otter, "the longer the trial is delayed the better, for it will give Badger and Miss Bugle time to travel back from the north."

So it was that by day the two river animals went about their normal business seemingly without concern for their incarcerated friends. While by night, unseen, they used their river skills to make passage to the boathouse, and put in place such provisions of food and clothing as their friends would need if they were to make a clean getaway.

Meanwhile, the mood in the Village regarding the prisoners changed from initial apathy to curiosity, then to excitement and finally, as the weasels and stoats began to take their guarding duties rather too seriously, to anger. For when they began to demand evidence of identity and purpose of travel, and then made the mistake of imposing a curfew after dark, the Villagers held a meeting at the Public House and an Action Committee was formed to free Mr Toad and Mr Mole.

As a result, two of those gentlemen the Mole had met in the Public House before Christmas, having heard of Ratty and Otter's sterling work trying to defend the prisoners from their enemies at Toad Hall on Christmas Day, called upon them on behalf of the Committee to solicit their support.

This provided the breakthrough in intelligence that the Rat needed, for when he heard that one of the Committee had actually been incarcerated in the Gaol and knew the layout of the inside of the Court House they quickly arranged to meet him. He told them all he knew and for the first time they saw that there might be a means of freeing their friends.

It was now the third of January, and the tenth night of the prisoners' incarceration was approaching. That same day the Rat gained new intelligence that made it imperative that their friends were sprung from gaol as soon as possible – the date of their trial had been set.

They learned this in the form of a notice brought from the Village by the Action Committee, which had been posted far and wide.

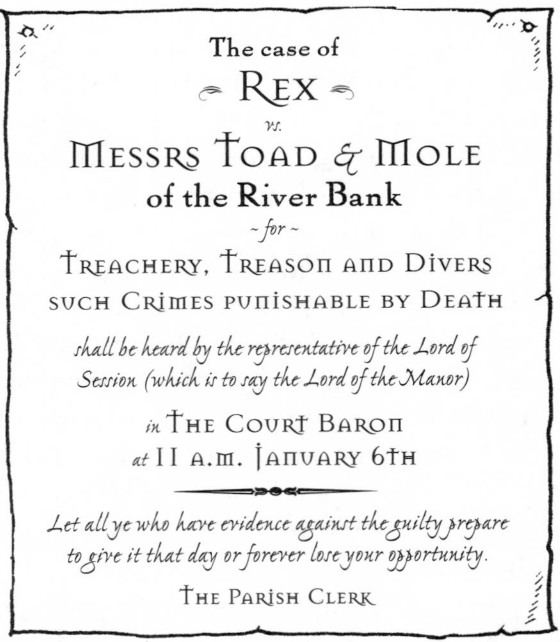

The case of

REX

vs.

MESSRS TOAD & MOLE

of the River Bank

~ for ~

TREACHERY, TREASON AND DIVERS SUCH CRIMES PUNISHABLE BY DEATH

shall be heard by the representative of the Lord of Session (which is to say the Lord of the Manor)

in THE COURT BARON

at 11 A.M. JANUARY 6TH

Let all ye who have evidence against the guilty prepare to give it that day or forever lose your opportunity.

THE PARISH CLERK

"We shall have to make our move at once," declared the Rat when he heard this news. "I beg you to return at once to our friends on the Action Committee and ask them to create a diversion in the Village at ten o'clock tonight to give us the opportunity to get Toad and Mole out unseen!"

"You have a plan then?" asked the Villager.

"In a manner of speaking, we have," said the Water Rat evasively, "but we had best keep it secret, even from you."

"Well, this is exciting!" said their ally. "A diversion there will be!"

When he had gone, the Otter looked at the Rat and said, "It certainly *is* exciting, since you have even kept your 'plan' secret from me!"

The Rat sank despondently into his armchair and said gloomily, "There is no plan, you know that as well as I, but perhaps if we make one last attempt, inspiration might come..."

The Water Rat had long since realized that the only way of rescuing his friends without breaking down the door was by way of the culvert that dropped from their cell straight into the river. It was this seemingly impossible route – which no prisoner had ever used in the Pound's five-hundred-year history, and survived – that had so taxed Rat's ingenuity these days past. But after two hours of uninspired debate, they found they had made no further progress.

Morning gave way to afternoon and after a late lunch the Rat said suddenly, "You know, I remember Mole telling me once that when he is stumped by some problem or other he resorts to a glass or two of his famous sloe and blackberry. He feels it is inclined to loosen the mind."

The Otter needed no second bidding. He went to the Rat's kitchen cupboard, found an opened bottle of that remarkable brew and poured two glasses. They supped it in silence as the precious minutes continued to slip away. After a second glass the Rat felt his head begin to spin and he realized he must drink no more if he was to have a clear mind for the evening.

"Let us try one more time," said the Rat. "Now, we agree that the culvert offers the only escape?"

The Otter nodded.

"We agree that while you or I can hold our breath underwater long enough to swim from the bank and up into the culvert, it is no good expecting an animal as cowardly and inclined to panic as Toad to emulate the feat in the opposite direction?"

"Nor is it sensible to hope that one as unused to swimming as Mole, however brave he may be – and we know he is – might attempt this escape without help from one of us."

"Hmmm," mused the Rat, before adding, "mind you, our good friend Mole has surprised us on many an occasion with his resourcefulness and bravery, so we should not now underestimate his ability to help us and himself in this situation."

More silence followed till, sighing with resignation and his face filled with a look of reluctant defeat, the Rat quaffed the last of the sloe and blackberry and slowly got to his feet.

"Rat, old chap, if even you cannot think of a way then there surely is none!" said the Otter sombrely.

"I really don't like to give up when I know that Toad and Mole are relying on us, but you know, Otter, sometimes we simply have to accept that there is no solution, and that … and that … that … *that's it!*"

He turned about the room several times, glass still in his hand, in a state of considerable excitement.

"What's *it*?" cried the Otter, relieved to see the light of inventive insight in the Rat's eyes.

"This, old fellow, *this...*" cried the Rat, holding up his glass for the Otter to see before turning it upside down and placing it on top of his head.

When the Otter still seemed not to understand, the normally sensible Water Rat began to walk about the room with the glass balanced precariously on his head while extending his hands and arms in front of him and sweeping them about as if removing unseen cobwebs.

It was suddenly all too plain to the Otter that his most trustworthy of friends had suddenly gone mad, driven to that state by worry for their friends, and the effort of thinking too hard.

"Yes, yes..." cried the Rat, making exaggerated movements of his legs, and narrowing his eyes in a fierce and ferocious way, as if fighting his way through thick undergrowth, "this is it!"

He is not only mad, thought the Otter, *but very likely will soon become dangerous as well!*

"Rat," essayed the concerned Otter in a gentle way, as one might talk to someone who is likely to turn violent if spoken to too harshly or suddenly, "you look rather tired. Perhaps it would be wise if you went to bed for an hour or two and rested so that you awaken refreshed and feeling better."

"Tired?" cried the Rat in surprise, taking the glass off his head. "*Better?* I never felt less tired than I do now, and never better. But having solved the problem of getting Toad and Mole out of the Village Gaol in principle, I must work out how to carry through the solution in practice. I had rather hoped you might have something to contribute, Otter, but if you're tired then by all means go to bed and leave me to it!"

He turned his back on the bemused Otter and disappeared into his kitchen, from whence his friend soon heard the sound of running water and the clatter of metal pans. The Otter was just contemplating his options, one of which was flight, when he heard the Rat calling out to him in an otherworldly, muffled kind of voice.

Fearing that the demented Rat might cause himself injury, the good-hearted Otter rushed to his aid. He found his friend amidst a scatter of ancient and long unused cooking equipment. Over his head and quite covering it up, he held a metal tureen of such vast proportions that it could only have been one used in the distant past for cooking stews for a troop of soldiers, or perhaps for a hog's head, whole.

"Well?" said the Rat. "Do you think it will do?"

"It looks very well on you, old fellow," said the Otter even more gently than before, his eyes searching for something with which to defend himself.

"Looks well on me!" cried the Rat as he advanced upon the Otter and bumped into the table. "I am not concerned with looks but practicalities!"

He took the tureen off his head and seemed very

"Hold on to him," cried the Water Rat... *(p. 196)*

surprised to find that the Otter had adopted a position of defence, a serrated bread knife in one hand and a cast-iron frying pan in the other. Light dawned upon the Rat's face and he eyed the Otter quizzically.

"My dear fellow," said he, starting to chuckle, "I am beginning to think you have not quite followed my drift."

"Well..." said the Otter uneasily and not yet dropping his guard, "your behaviour seems decidedly odd, to say the least of it, and I really think you should allow me to summon help."

"Look here," said the Rat, chuckling even as he put down the tureen and took up the glass once more. "Perhaps I had presumed too much in thinking you understood my plan! Now, see what happens if we invert this glass and put it in the water in my sink, so. The air is trapped inside as I push it underwater, leaving sufficient to breathe for anyone whose head is inside such a vessel. Of course, it needs to be bigger than a glass – hence the tureen."

"Well I never!" cried the Otter who saw the implications at once. "You think we might take these through the culvert and persuade Toad and Mole to escape with tureens on their heads to help them breathe?"

"That's about the size of it," said the Rat.

"Do you have a second tureen?"

"This one will do for Toad, for his head is very big, and somewhere or other I have a pan I used to use for jam-making, before Mole came to the River Bank and took it upon himself to supply me with jam and other conserves."

He found the pan and set it alongside the other.

"But will it work?" mused the Otter.

"It will, provided one does not allow the vessel holding the air to tilt too much, for if you do..."

He tilted the glass, the air escaped in two or three bubbles, and water immediately rushed in to replace it.

"Hmm. We'd better test it ourselves," said the Rat.

"Capital!" cried the Otter.

Taking a length of rope from his boathouse, the Rat tied it about his waist and, giving the loose end to the Otter, clambered down the muddy bank till his ankles were in the water.

"Hand me down the tureen, there's a good fellow," he sang out, "and if I tug at the rope three times haul me in without further ado. Otherwise, be sure to let it out so that I may make what progress I can under the water, and don't worry if I am longer than you expect. Time is slower for those who watch than for those who do."

With this philosophical thought the Rat placed the tureen over his head, held fast to its handles with each hand, and boldly waded through the muddy water. The Otter watched with very mixed feelings and his heart gave a jolt when, with a muffled cry of farewell, the Rat disappeared beneath the water.

The glint of the submerged tureen was soon lost to view and the rope pulled away from the Otter's hands erratically. The Otter was tempted to haul him in at once, or better still dive in and rescue him, but he recognized that the experiment was for Toad and the Mole's benefit rather than their own. After all, he and the Water Rat were such expert swimmers that they had no need of air supplies.

Eventually, after an uncomfortably long wait, and astonished that the Rat could still find air to breathe, the Otter saw the tureen break the surface of the water near the other bank. Letting forth an involuntary cheer, he watched as his friend took the tureen off his head and turned to wave most cheerfully.

Shortly afterwards, as he dried off in his house and changed his clothes, the Water Rat told the Otter of the experience.

"I couldn't see anything at all, of course, unless I pulled my head out of the vessel and looked about. That's why I stumbled a couple of times. But where the river flows in the Village the bottom is clear and gravelly and even Toad should be able to find a footing. We must be practical, however. I doubt that we will be able to persuade Toad to set forth from his cell into the culvert willingly, so between us the Mole and I will have to force him."

"I could come and help too," said the Otter.

The Rat shook his head. "No, I want you to stay nearby with the boat we secreted away near the Village against such an eventuality as this. But we must blacken it so that the guards don't see it..."

"I've done that already," said the excellent Otter.

"Good fellow. Now then, when we get out you can help Toad and Mole aboard, and we can make our getaway. I think it might be wise to take some flotation aids for Mole and Toad, for the river by the Gaol runs fast and if they lose their footing they might be glad of some artificial help. I have just the thing..."

He went back into the boathouse and emerged moments later with some pigs' bladders, which he kept as an aid to winter fishing. Then they made their final preparations and set out for the Village as darkness fell, to recover the boat and position themselves in good time for the rescue attempt.

It was a cold night and the two animals were chilled to the bone by the time they heard the clock of the Village church strike ten. But they did not have to wait long for evidence of the diversion.

The members of the Committee, acting on the Rat's instruction to the letter, adopted the stratagem of extending their normal bar-room merriment to the street outside, and there allowing matters to get so out of hand that it soon became a brawl. When nearby weasels and stoats tried to restore order, the brawl turned nasty, and other guards, including those watching over Toad and the Mole, had to be hastily summoned.

Their departure was the signal the resourceful Rat had waited for, and he slipped out of the rescue boat into the rushing river, with a bag containing the tureen, the jam pan and assorted pigs' bladders on his back.

The Mole and Toad were fast asleep when the Rat

appeared in the culvert below the cell and called up to them. He did so as quietly as he could against the rush of the water in the hope that the Mole would wake first, for otherwise the alarmed Toad might easily have given the game away.

"Is that really you, Ratty?" whispered a very nervous Mole into the watery gloom below.

"It is," whispered the Rat, "and I've come to get you out of here. Now listen, Mole, this is not a time for niceties but resolute action…"

He quickly told Mole the plan, warning him that they must find a way of getting Toad into the noisome culvert, and quickly.

"Once you've got him down here leave me to do the rest," said the Rat grimly.

The Mole nodded and contemplated Toad, upon whose face was a happy smile that suggested he was dreaming of former glories, or of wonderful meals in the world's best hotels.

"Toad," said the Mole urgently, shaking him awake, "I've found a way out of here."

Toad sat up woozily.

"Come and look… quickly, over here."

The still sleepy Toad meekly did as he was told and peered down into the culvert.

"What am I meant to see?"

It was at such moments as this, when decisive action was needed, that the normally quiet and modest Mole surprised the other River Bankers. Without more ado, not even an apology, he placed his hand firmly in the small of Toad's back, and shoved him over the culvert's edge and down into the waiting arms of the Rat.

As Toad let out a cry, as of one whose dream seems about to turn into a nightmare, the Rat caught him, tied an inflated pig's bladder to each of his four limbs and cried out to the Mole, "Wait down here till my return!" Then he thrust the tureen on to the bewildered Toad's head and bodily pulled him down into the water and away through the underwater stone arches of the ancient culvert.

Toad was suddenly aware that his body was very wet and very cold, and his extremities were being pulled in different directions by strange balloons attached with twine, and that in his ears was the rushing sound of water on metal. Certain that he was having a nightmare, he began to fight off his attackers.

As the Rat and he broke the water's surface, which they did as a cork might burst from a vigorously shaken champagne bottle by virtue of the upward pull of the too-eager bladders, they very nearly capsized the waiting rescue vessel and threw the Otter into the water.

"Hold on to him," cried the Water Rat, thrusting the struggling Toad to the side of the boat, "I'm going back for Mole."

As Toad began a relentless assault on his second rescuer, shouting for help as he did so, and running the danger of attracting the attention of those very guards they had been hoping to evade, the brave Rat plunged back into the depths. He effected the Mole's rescue as sweetly as extracting the last pea from its pod, and the Mole and he reappeared on the surface with plenty of air left in the jam pan – so much indeed that the Mole was rather reluctant to let it go as the Rat pulled him towards the boat, for there was a certain novelty to the situation that he rather enjoyed.

Of the chaotic moments that followed not even a Royal Commission of Enquiry could establish the full and absolute truth, were it to spend twenty years doing so.

Of the participants themselves, the Otter remembered trying to wrest a heavy metal rowlock from Toad's grasp; the Rat remembered the Otter falling forward upon the Mole; the Mole remembered their rescue craft capsizing right on top of him, and Toad remembered, quite distinctly, a nightmare he had had, which turned into an heroic dream, in which he, brave, brilliant and resourceful as ever, had the brilliant idea of rescuing all three of his friends with pigs' bladders and letting the river's rapid flow float them away from the dark, dank walls of the Gaol, and from there, under cover of night and all unseen, right through the Village, past the church, and away to liberty.

Thus began an escapade that was very soon to be described in the national press as rivalling the *Marie Celeste* for mystery, the *Prisoner of Zenda* for daring, and the *Scarlet Pimpernel*, in the form of Toad, for its hero.

When the Rat, the Otter and the Mole had recovered their senses, and restored the now gibbering Toad to some form of normality, they made their way to the boathouse on Toad's estate. By the time they had dried themselves off, warmed themselves up and gained a little rest, the sun was rising.

Only then did the Parish Clerk and the minions of the Court discover the appalling truth: the birds had flown, and nobody knew how. The gentlemen of the press descended in very short order upon the Village, and in no time at all the visages of Toad and his accomplice in crime, the Mole, were emblazoned on the front page of every newspaper in the land, along with various offers of reward, not least a very substantial one from the ticket touts who stood to lose a great deal of money if the trial did not take place as planned.

Although the reports universally condemned Toad for his actions, the fact was that they could not help portraying him as a hero – and a victim too.

Headlines such as TOAD ESCAPES! were soon replaced by TOAD ESCAPES TO PROVE HIS INNOCENCE. Followed by IS TOAD A SECRET AGENT? And then I AM INNOCENT!!! TOAD'S OWN STORY.

These fabrications added fuel to the fire of interest in Toad and Mole that swept the land, and was the sole source of conversation and debate from Lords' libraries to tramps' park benches; from emporia serving the better classes to those dark taverns serving the lowest.

Thus it was that two days later, having moved from Toad's boathouse to a safe retreat on the River near the outskirts of the Town lent to them by a boating friend of the Rat, the two fugitives remained in hiding. The Rat and the Otter had long since realized that if they were not to be accused of being party to the escape they must be back in their own homes the day after it.

"You have enough food to lie low for days without showing your faces," the Rat told Toad and the Mole. "Do not go out or let yourselves be seen. Mole, make sure temptation does not come Toad's way. Let him see no motor-cars, no motor-launches, no flying machines – *nothing* that will lead him into temptation."

The Mole nodded, more confident of his success because Toad's friends had deemed it in his best interests to handcuff him to a chain attached to a pillar in the basement of their hiding place. There he might cry out all he liked, but he would be safe.

For two days, and with just one more to go before the trial was due to start, the Mole listened to Toad's pleas and entreaties that he might be released, but remained firm. He plied his friend with food and comforting words, and said again and again that it was in their best interests that he stayed where he was.

"I wish only to breathe the fresh air of liberty," said Toad. "Only to stretch my limbs into the firmament of freedom! Only to set my eyes upon the sunlight of hope! Only to… ha! ha!… got you, Mole!"

"Let me go!" cried the Mole, who in a single unguarded moment found the chain wrapped round him, his keys taken, the handcuffs loosened and replaced upon himself, and the thoughtless and ungrateful Toad climbing the stairs towards the world outside and leaving him in darkness.

"Toad, do not be so foolish!" cried the Mole. "Set me free at once!"

Toad made no reply, but skipped lightly through the outside door of their retreat, and headed off in the direction of the Town.

Being confined was never an easy thing for Toad and he had grown bored with the Mole's conversation. If only he had freed him then what fun they might have had, but as he had refused, what else could a Toad do?

Thinking such thoughts, and dressed in the garb of a low type which the Rat had thought might be the best disguise, Toad soon found that wandering the streets was not to his liking. He needed sustenance. He needed company. He needed an audience.

It alarmed him greatly to see the many "WANTED"

signs that bore his image, and that of the Mole. He pulled his cap over his head and thought he would probably be better disguised in the dark, smoky atmosphere of a tavern, where he might also get some food.

The ever-practical Rat had provided both fugitives with cash, little thinking what dangerous use Toad would put it to.

"What d'yer want?" said the landlord.

"Boiled beef an' carrerts," said Toad in that rough accent he liked to adopt in such situations. "An' a jug o' yer best."

The beer was quickly drawn, the food soon served, and the happy Toad found himself sitting in the shadows of an inglenook by a roaring fire, while the rest of the low clientele carried on with their own business.

It was only when he had eaten his food and had a slice of lardy cake as well as another jug of the best, that he harkened to the conversation of his fellow revellers. He was astonished and delighted to hear they were talking about him and his remarkable escape. What was more, they were doing so in words of respect and admiration!

The mystery of the escape remained unsolved and the Town's evening paper had offered a special reward to anyone who could come up with a satisfactory explanation of how Mr Toad of Toad Hall had effected his brilliant escape.

"He didn't do it on his tod but 'ad 'elp," said one; "that's for certain."

"Official 'elp, if you ask me," said another.

"It's generally agreed 'e's an agent, but fer 'oo, that's the question."

"Yeh, but just supposin' 'e didn't 'ave 'elp, 'ow could 'e get out of his cell and leave no trace?"

"Well, actually, it wasn't so difficult…" began Toad before he realized what he was doing.

"Not difficult?" said one near him. "I suppose you know how it was done then!"

There was a general laugh at this and all eyes turned on Toad.

"No, honestly, I haven't, I mean I 'aven't no notion of wot 'appened."

"Well, mate, if you did 'ave this paper 'ere would give you a hundred pounds in cash if you tell 'em how."

Another drinker held up the paper in question, which had a picture of Toad for all to see. Toad pulled his cap lower down his face, and held his beer close to him to add to his disguise.

"One thing's certain, that Mr Toad's the greatest toad wot ever lived. 'E's cocked a snook at authority like we all would like to do. 'E must be the cleverest criminal that ever was."

"To Mr Toad," cried another, raising his glass, "in the hope we might meet 'im one day and shake 'is 'and."

Once more Toad's natural vanity and desire for applause briefly got the better of him and he rose as if to reply to the toast.

"Gentlemen," he began, "I… I…" and then he sat down again with a thump.

Too late! For once more all eyes were on him and before their cheerful gaze Toad felt what he had not felt for many long days and nights – the thrill of others wanting to hear what he had to say.

"Don't be bashful, chum," said another, "if you want to speechify in 'onour of Mr Toad there's none 'ere will stop you!"

That word "speechify" was like nectar to Toad, as were the shouts of others in his audience of "Speech! Speech!"

"Well then," began Toad, quite forgetting himself and the danger he was in, "I think I may offer you an explanation of how the great Mr Toad and his feeble-minded accomplice Mr Mole escaped."

Silence fell.

"'E's got inside information," whispered one.

"'E looks like a member of the Albert gang," said another in an awed voice, for that gang was known to be the most vicious and dangerous in the Town, and its name had been attached to the escape.

"I do indeed have inside information," said Toad, his chest swelling, "and I can tell you exactly how the most audacious, most cleverly conceived, most memorable escape from a locked cell was done, without breaking the locks!"

Complete silence had now fallen among the cognoscenti of the tavern as they pushed forward to hear the speaker – the more so because rumours had spread rapidly to the furthest reaches of the tavern to the effect that Mr Albert 'imself, leader of the Albert gang, was even now spilling the beans on Mr Toad's escape in the front bar.

Toad waxed eloquent, describing the escape in detail, making clear that at each stage Mr Toad showed great bravery, the more so because of the necessity of helping his weaker accomplice Mr Mole, who as the papers had frequently pointed out, was not of Mr Toad's calibre, and indeed was as weak of brain as he was of body.

"Mr Albert," cried one of his listeners to Toad during a brief recess while Toad gratefully accepted the offer of further liquid refreshment, "'ow do you know all this if–?"

"Who's Mr Albert?" asked Toad, not quite liking the idea of someone else muscling in on his patch.

The matter was quickly explained, and with many a nod and wink Toad's new friends gave him to understand that they knew he was Mr Albert but his secret was safe with them.

This mistaken identity somewhat offended Toad, but as he resumed his account he felt it wisest not to react to it, for it would keep his disguise all the better. So it was that Toad continued to inflate himself in public, adding falsehood to fabrication to make himself appear ever more heroic, ever more brilliant and ever more beyond the reach of the law.

It was a pity, therefore, that when one of his listeners persisted in calling him Mr Albert, and worse, suggested that he, Mr Albert, was perhaps a braver person in many ways than Toad, that Toad's common sense finally gave way. He had not seen the people who had recently appeared at the tavern door, dressed in the blue and silver-button garb of constables.

"Gentlemen," cried Toad, "I have one last secret to reveal before I must away!"

With that he took his cap off and said, "No Albert am I, but Toad himself, here honouring you with his flesh and blood. Applaud me, honour me, but never attempt

to do what I have done, for without my skill and brilliance you are bound to get caught!"

Toad could not resist holding up the newspaper with his image on its front page to prove what all there knew was true the moment he removed his cap.

"Strike a light!" cried one.

"Stap me vitals," said another.

"Mr Albert *is* Mr Toad," said a third.

"Arrest that Toad!" cried a police officer, and the constables charged Toad and after a brief struggle took him into custody.

Soon afterwards, the police moved in to arrest Mole where Toad had left him. But that sterling creature, realizing what a parlous position he was in and rightly thinking that in such a case prudence was the better part of valour, had secured his own release by using the spare key he kept in his waistcoat pocket. Then he had searched for Toad and, observing him in the tavern, realized at once the likely outcome and hidden outside against the vain hope that Toad might get away with it.

But he did not, and when the Mole saw him thrust into a Black Maria, surrounded by armed guards, he knew that for Toad the game was up. For himself, his only recourse was to make his solitary way by riverside and hedgerow back towards the River Bank, there to try to contact the Rat once again and see what they might do.

· XI ·
Lord of the Manor

The trial of Toad of Toad Hall was due to start at eleven o'clock in the morning on the sixth of January, but for the assembled mob it began an hour earlier when the prisoner was brought in irons up the steps from his cell below the bridge, and thence to the Court House.

"There he be, the villain!" many cried.

"Can yer see 'im, Alfie, 'e's on 'is way to 'is doom?!" cried another, hoisting his child up on to his shoulder to get a better look.

"Ladies and gentlemen," began Toad when the press became so close that the constables who had now taken charge of him were brought to a halt, "may I take this opportunity of thanking you for coming today, because I want to say that –"

"Wot's 'e on abaht?" cried one.

"Madam," said Toad, "what I am on about, as you put it, is this –"

But whatever it was, no one ever knew, for the hapless Toad was swiftly escorted through the throng and hauled into the Court House. There he was secured in a cage of iron bars set especially in the antechamber so that those who had paid 2/6d or more for their seats might have a preliminary view.

It was only then, as the crowd peered at him as they might some wild and exotic beast in the Town's Zoological Gardens, that poor Toad began to understand the true nature of his awful plight.

There before him were the signs on the three great doors that Mole had seen during his visit before Christmas: "Legal Gentlemen and Witnesses", "The Judge" and finally "The Condemned".

It was the last one that brought Toad's spirit low and caused him to slump down on the metal stool, which was the only furniture in his cage.

"'E's stopped speakin' and 'e's sittin'!"

"'E's thinkin'."

Toad saw only their feet, for he was suddenly too fearful, too daunted, to look up.

"The Condemned," it said, and that he must surely be. He was alone, without friends, without hope.

"Toad!"

Then again, *"TOAD!"*

He looked up in astonishment, for the voice he heard was none other than Mole's!

"Toad, it's me!"

Toad blinked in astonishment, but had the presence of mind not to give the game away. For there was Mole, and near him Ratty, and not far off Otter, in the disguise of peasant yeomanry.

"*We shan't desert you, Toad. We shall find a way to get you free, I'm sure we shall!"*

It was all the Mole had time to whisper before the crowd surged forward and he felt it best to sink back into it to avoid being noticed and recognised.

Toad could hardly believe it. "Mole – here!"

Nothing could have lifted his spirits more than to think that the Mole was risking recapture just to give him moral support. Ratty and Otter too!

Toad was oppressed no more. He rose up, climbed on to his metal stool, clutched the bars and addressed the baying crowd: "You see before you one who has been wrongfully accused and who..."

"Hush – 'e's stopped thinkin' and 'e's speakin' again."

"Ssh! Let's 'ear wot a villain says afore 'e meets 'is maker!"

"... one who stands trial on behalf of the oppressed folk of the Village!" continued Toad, his voice growing in confidence as the crowd fell silent, "Oppressed, I say, and broken!"

"'E's just –" began a weasel dismissively.

"Give 'im a chance," said a Villager, "give 'im an 'earin'."

"Broken and beaten are those who live in the Village. But I shall not be broken or beaten so long as there are Villagers brave enough to come here to support me today!"

"Hear! Hear!" cried a Villager who had earlier been distributing rotten eggs and tomatoes from a basket for the crowd to throw at Toad.

"You, sir," cried Toad, who like all demagogues on such occasions could be most impressive provided the quality of the thoughts expressed were not too closely attended to, "I ask you – I command you – to hurl those items of war not at me but at the weasels and stoats, who have sullied the Village with their presence!"

"We'll have rather less of that, sir, if you please," said the constable nearest Toad.

But it was too late, for the Village took Toad's words as commands and hurled the missiles at the intruders.

In no time at all there was uproar, and as a posse of constables moved in to restore order Toad was hastily released from his cage and removed by way of the door marked "The Condemned" into the Court Room itself. There he was placed in the dock and chained to a metal eye bolted to the top of the dock.

The Court Room was already half-filled with those gentlemen and ladies who had been able to afford the more expensive seats, and whose excitement had grown with the hubbub outside. When they saw Toad being escorted in they let out a strange gasp, and a good many ladies fainted right away to find themselves so close to such a villain.

His appearance seemed all the more criminal because a huge candle, of the kind normally used in church to light the way of sinners to holy communion, had been placed near the dock. It cast flickering shadows on Toad's face and though he tried to smile and look respectable, it had the unfortunate effect of making him look like a gargoyle.

There were other such candles placed about the Court, and three or four flares on metal posts, which were useful augmentation to the light that filtered in through the smoke and dust from the high windows above.

The Parish Clerk was robed in black, and wore a wig. He was seated below the Judge's Bench, with the dock to his right and near that, rather low down, a very few seats marked out as being for "Defence Witnesses". But nobody was sitting there for Toad.

On the Clerk's left hand, and facing the dock in such a way that their seats were elevated and formidable, were the Prosecution Witnesses. There were a good many of these, including the Chief Weasel, an ancient stoat and all the guests who had been at Mrs Ffleshe's fateful Christmas luncheon.

Most formidable of all was Mrs Ffleshe, dressed that day in regal green silk and with enough jewellery to show that she was a woman of consequence, but not so much that she seemed flamboyant. Her face was powdered and in consequence a little pale, her eyes wide and pathetic. In short she looked just as she intended to look – as if she had suffered terribly at the hands of the accused.

Mrs Ffleshe's hair, which was normally swept back in a severe style, had on this occasion been coiffured by a gentleman from Town who had softened its effect with ringlets and a chaste ribbon or two to match her dress. The effect of these contrivances was to make her more sympathetic to those who did not know her; to those who did, however, it was not far short of attempting to improve a wild, man-eating tigress from the jungles of Bengal by perching a dove of peace, stuffed, upon its head.

In the excitement caused by Toad's arrival and the sudden inrush of ticket-holders who had been lingering outside, the disguised Rat, Mole and Otter took their places unnoticed in the shadows of the higher and more distant seats.

Soon the Court Room grew quiet with mounting expectation, and some trepidation too. The work of the specialist craftsmen the Clerk had mentioned to Toad and Mole was not yet fully visible, for the instruments of trial to which the accused must soon be subjected in the interests of justice were covered with dust sheets.

They had been assembled in the well of the Court, which, with the extra seating now stacked up about it, had the appearance of a bear-baiting pit. Here a spiked metal wheel was visible, there a thumbscrew or two.

In one corner, like a grotesque mummy from an Egyptian tomb, the sheets covered an upright figure with head and shoulders and a bulky body. This, the cognoscenti knew, was the Iron Maiden into whose spiked and brutal interior the accused must be placed for his own good.

How very eagerly the sharp tines of the instruments of trial pushed through their coverings; how positively the pulleys peered out, and the arms and legs of the racks waved their greetings; and how welcoming the grinning teeth of the prods and rakes; and how pretty the tresses of the iron chains and manacles!

In one portion of this dreadful pit two muscular gentlemen, clad in leather and masked, were tending a brazier of coals, which was sending into the atmosphere the scent of fire, smoke and brimstone.

The only way into this place of trial was from a little door that opened out to one side of the dock; the only way out of it appeared to be those dreadful worn steps that the Mole had observed some days before, which led to the door set high in the Court Room wall, and whose egress he knew to be a fatal plunge into the torrent below.

Only one other part of the Court Room attracted as much attention as the doleful pit of trial, and that was the Royal Box adjacent to it. It had been a considerable disappointment to the crowd that it had thus far remained empty, but as they heard the first chimes of eleven from the nearby church tower, a door at its rear opened, from which there was a brief show of light illuminating four plush red seats as two figures ascended from a little stairway and the door closed again, putting the box back into darkness.

"It's 'im, it's the Prince!" cried several of the onlookers, and a mighty cheer spread about the Court. The Prince, a bulky gentleman, took a vantage point in his box from which he might view the proceedings, but, as royalty sometimes will, he stayed in the shadows, his servant at his side, their faces discreetly hidden so that the Judges might not be influenced by such expressions of support or contempt for the accused as they made.

When a spontaneous verse or two of the National Anthem was sung the Prince waved his hand in regal appreciation and seemed about to rise and bow when his servant put a restraining hand on his arm as if to say "Remember how Abraham Lincoln came to be assassinated and stay back in the safety of the box!" Then, with a nod towards the Parish Clerk, the Prince signalled that the proceedings should begin.

As the last stroke of eleven sounded the Parish Clerk banged his gavel and called everybody to order.

"Your Very Royal Highness, Lords, Ladies, Judges and Gentlemen, and ye yeomanry and tithe-payers of this Royal Village, mark ye that the Court Baron is now in session! Pray silence for the entry of the three Judges Nominal, namely Perspicacious, Purposeful and Pitiless, and His Lordship the Prosecuting Counsel!"

This was the signal for the entry of the Judges, all robed in black, followed by Lord Mallice, taller and gaunter than the others, who as Prosecuting Counsel sat with the Judges themselves.

One of the Judges took the central chair and he it was who spoke first, in a thin and aged voice.

"We are here to see justice done and we shall see it done. Remarks will be addressed to us as representative of the virtues of perspicacity in the affirmative, purposefulness in the neutral and pity in the negative. There being no counsel for the defence, the accused's crimes being so wretched and dreadful, I shall ask Lord Mallice to proceed forthwith."

"My Lords," said he at once as if there was not a moment to lose. "In the dock you see the accused whose name is written on this sheet of charges."

"*He* is Toad of Toad Hall?" said one of the Judges, eyeing him.

"He is," said Lord Mallice.

"Can he speak and identify himself?"

"I can speak and my name is Toad," said Toad in a firm voice which sent shivers down the spines of the ladies who had fainted earlier, "and since you ask, may I take this opportunity of saying a few words?"

"No you may not," said Lord Mallice, silencing Toad with a stare. "Parish Clerk, is the Court in order and its officials in place?"

"It is, My Lord," said the Parish Clerk in measured tones, "which is to say –"

"That is good," said Lord Mallice, sharply interrupting him to make quite plain he wished all replies to be brief.

"How does the accused plead?" enquired one of the Judges.

Toad swelled his chest and looked about him, readying himself for his first major speech.

"Guilty or not guilty?" enquired another Judge.

"I was about to come to that, My Lordships," said Toad, rising to the task, "because when I think about the word 'guilty' and ponder the word 'innocent', it certainly seems to me that –"

"Enter a guilty plea," said the Judge Purposeful with impatience, "but let's try him all the same."

Ignoring Toad's attempts to speak, the Parish Clerk dipped his quill into a bottle of black ink and intoned, "G for Guilt, E for Even more guilt, U for Under a stone as in come from, I for not Innocent, T for Telling me! and Y for You, Mr Toad. Which is to say, 'Guilty'."

The crowd clapped this performance loudly and the Judges nodded their heads approvingly.

"My Lords," said Lord Mallice, "since the charges against this criminal are so many and varied, but all capital, I suggest we call the chief witness at once and proceeding from her testimony seek to discover through trials and tribulations of the condemned whether her evidence is true, and if so waste no more of the Court's time than is necessary to satisfy us all that the prisoner is guilty *prima facie,* and if so – and it is our contention it will be – we may proceed at once to the second and final trial, which is execution, subject to your Lordships' preferences as to manner, type, category and circumstance."

"Agreed," said the Judges.

"Call Mrs Ffleshe of Toad Hall," said the Parish Clerk.

Mrs Ffleshe, sighing heavily, weeping profusely and in need of support on both sides, was led into the witness box, where she was given a chair with a silk cushion and a decanter of water.

Her painful progress was the subject of silent and sympathetic scrutiny by the crowd, so that by the time she had sat down there was considerable unrest and a good many shouts of deprecation were aimed at Toad.

"Yer a brute for doin' this to a fine lady!"

"Her bravery's a match fer your cowardice any day!"

"Brute?" cried Toad, rising despite his manacles. "Why, that lady is –"

"The prisoner will be silent," said the Judge Pitiless.

Toad subsided and stared at Mrs Ffleshe.

"Madam," said the Judge Purposeful, "are you quite ready for cross-examination?"

"I am, sir," said Mrs Ffleshe in a weak and trembling voice, "as ready as I can ever be after what this – this gentleman has done to me. But I shall do my best."

"We're wiv you, ducks!" cried a female voice in the crowd. "You tell 'em!" cried another.

Mrs Ffleshe looked sadly in their direction and acknowledged their support with a brief smile that was heartbreaking for the simple courage it showed.

"Dear madam," began Lord Mallice, looming high.

"O, My Lord," whispered Mrs Ffleshe.

"Will you –"

"I will!"

"Madam, I know you are overwrought," said the Judge Perspicacious, "but please try to wait till Counsel's question is complete."

"Yes, sir," said Mrs Ffleshe meekly, her adoring eyes upon Lord Mallice.

"I repeat, Mrs Ffleshe, will you tell the Court in your own words how you first came to be at Toad Hall?"

"I came to help *him*, to save him from himself, after he forced my mother, a weak and defenceless lady of advanced age, a nanny by vocation, a lover of children, a woman of sympathy, to work for him all hours of the day and night. I came and was made subjugate myself, forced to do unspeakable things..."

"Dearest lady, if it is too painful for you to mention these unspeakable things then we can take them as read and put the prisoner to ordeal at once."

"Painful, yes; impossible, no! Somebody must have the courage to speak out. I had to clean out grates..."

There was a gasp at this from the better class of ladies in the crowd.

"... and haul in coals ..."

"The cad!" cried a gentleman.

"... and scrub the flagstone floors with a toothbrush!"

"That be the next best thing to torture be that!" said a Village lady.

"And this with only one meal a week and that eaten outside in the rain! My mother grew frail with worry and yet still she dared not complain for fear he would do again what he did before, which – which –"

As Mrs Ffleshe kept up this farrago of nonsense the crowd began to hurl ever worse insults at Toad, while his attempts to defend himself were all cut short by Lord Mallice and the Judges together.

"O, my dear madam," said Lord Mallice with feeling, "I am sure I speak for all when I say that never has a court in this land had to listen to such a catalogue of cruelty to a lady of such ineffable – such charmingly – such –"

"And yet, My Lord," cried Mrs Ffleshe with passion, readying herself for her *pièce de résistance*, "I now beg and plead with the

Court not to punish him, but to let him free, for he knows not what he does!"

"What!" cried Lord Mallice astonished, and seemingly overwhelmed. "Is the witness saying that after everything that this … this …"

"Scum?" cried someone from the crowd.

"Slug?" cried another.

"Socialist!" cried a third.

"… that after everything this … gentleman has done, you still have it in your great heart to forgive him?"

"I have, my sweet Lord – set him free!"

"O, madam," said Lord Mallice, "I have never heard so affecting a plea. It is as if a little babe, having been struck down by a drunken and cruel brute, yet stands up in her holy innocence and cries 'Papa, I forgive you!'"

Lord Mallice, to whom tears were as alien as a monsoon in the Sahara, pulled a handkerchief from his pocket and affected to wipe away a tear.

"My Lord Pitiless," he said, handing him his kerchief, "use mine, I beg you!" For that Judge was now weeping openly at what he had heard, as were many of the crowd.

Throughout this last tirade Toad had wisely said nothing. But there was a look of incredulity on his face born first of Mrs Ffleshe's brazen lies, and second that the crowd should have been taken in by them.

"Toad of Toad Hall," said the Judge Perspicacious, "the charges against you are so serious and the evidence we have heard so strong that of itself it condemns you to penal servitude for seventy-five years with no remission after you have been executed, but I suppose we must hear your side of the story for form's sake.

"Lord Mallice, pray ask the prisoner the Dolorous Question and may the Court know that upon his reply will his ordeal depend. But please, I beg you, let us make it brief."

"I understand, My Lord," said Lord Mallice, looking at his pocket watch and seeing it was nearly time for lunch.

"Mr Toad, I must now ask you the Dolorous Question. Are you ready?"

"Well, I mean to say, old chap," spluttered Toad, "I might be ready if I knew exactly *what* the Dolorous Question was."

"I shall ask it and we shall see if you do," said Lord Mallice acidly.

A silence fell on the Court so profound that the pattering of a mouse's feet might be heard, and indeed *was* heard.

"Well then, Mr Toad, did you, or did you not?" asked Lord Mallice.

"I beg your pardon?" asked Toad.

"Did you, or did you not?"

"Did I *what*?" asked the exasperated Toad.

The gasp from the crowd and the Judges' shaking heads indicated that this was not the reply most favourable to him.

"I say again," cried Lord Mallice, "did you –?"

"Well, I *might* have done, I suppose," essayed the reluctant Toad once more.

Three ladies and a bishop's wife fainted, and two gentlemen too, while a third, whose voice had been heard before, cried out, "You're not only a cad, but a bounder too!"

"But then again I might not have done," said Toad, trying to recover lost ground, "because – because –"

He was now grasping at straws and not finding many.

"Because what?" asked Lord Mallice, a triumphant look in his eye such as a scorpion sports when it has its prey vulnerable before it and believes it cannot get away.

"Because," said Toad, his voice calm now, "I *had* to."

This astonishing assertion caught Lord Mallice unawares, and the Judges too. All four opened their mouths in blank astonishment.

"Yes," said Toad, "not only that, but I am certain, *positively* certain, that there is not a gentleman or a lady in this Court who in such a circumstance might not have done the same!"

"He *is* a villain!" cried a voice. "That's quite certain."

"But a clever one!" observed the Judge Perspicacious.

"Very!" said Purposeful.

"But not quite clever enough," observed Pitiless.

"My case rests, My Lords," said Lord Mallice. "May we now proceed to trial by ordeal?"

"But I have something else to say," said the desperate Toad.

"You have said it, prisoner, and most eloquently, for which reason we are giving you the opportunity for ordeal sooner rather than later."

"That is very kind, My Lord, but –" said Toad, his voice faltering.

At the word "ordeal" the two gentlemen in the pit had begun to remove the drapes and sheets and the crowd fell utterly silent once more, fascinated by the emergence into view of the machines infernal.

"He *is* a villain," cried a voice. "That's quite certain." *(p. 222)*

The two gentlemen, still masked, stood to attention by the rack and said, "Permission to speak, *sir*!"

"Granted."

"Deathwatch reporting for duty, sir!"

"And Beadle, *sir*! All present, working and ready, *sir*!"

They shouted so loud that dust fell from the hammer-beam roof above.

"Proceed," said the Judge Pitiless.

One of the constables guarding Toad opened the gate from the dock and Toad was ushered down. To his great credit he did not struggle, or shout, and showed no fear.

Instead he said, "My lords, ladies and gentlemen!"

"That is enough, prisoner, your silence will be more eloquent than your words."

"Shall we rack 'im, spit 'im, hang 'im or burn 'im, *sir*?"

"Clerk, do the statutes ordain an order for the trials?"

"They do, My Lords, my word they do. The entire proceedings are void and defunct if the trials proceed in the wrong order, which is to say, for example, that racking is after spitting which comes before tining but not after pronging, any one of which if carried out too soon or too late gives the prisoner right of protest."

"We see," said the three Judges simultaneously. "Which is the first ordained trial?"

"I would not advise axing," said the Parish Clerk, "for that is so serious a mis-ordering that the prisoner gets off scot-free after it, always providing he can pick himself up off the ground to make his protest, as it were. The *first*, since you ask, is boiling."

"Boiling let it be!" said Pitiless.

Deathwatch and Beadle grasped Toad by the arms and hoisting him clean off his legs bore him to a great vat of water beneath which a small fire was sending out feeble flames. As they dropped him in with a splash, there was a sudden gasp from the crowd.

Toad had closed his eyes when he was put in but opened them after a moment and splashed about a little.

"Hmm. It is rather tepid, in the manner of the Ritz, in Paris," he observed, as one who was a connoisseur of such things.

"Wot's tepid?" asked one of the crowd, speaking for many.

"Not quite hot enough, nor quite cold enough," replied Toad helpfully.

Toad looked at the Judges and they looked at him, and then all of them looked expectantly at Messrs Deathwatch and Beadle.

"We 'ad trouble with the logs wot is damp, me ludships, *sir!*" said Deathwatch.

"The prisoner is excused the boiling," said the Judge Purposeful. "Parish Clerk, what's next?"

"Racking, My Lords, which is to say stretching and pulling."

"Rack him," said Pitiless.

Deathwatch and Beadle, anxious to show that their equipment could perform rather better this time, hoisted the now dripping Toad out of the vat of tepid water and laid him on the rack, putting each of his wrists through a harsh metal loop.

"The left side's not quite tight enough," said Toad. Then, after a moment or two, he added, "No, that's the *right*, my man – I said the *left*. But come to think of it the right's not too good either. My dear chap, why don't you simply let me hold on to it – for I once played the pianoforte and my grip is really quite good – and then you can fasten my feet and we will all see if it works."

"'E's a cool one," said a member of the crowd with admiration.

"A bounder but a calm bounder," said the one who had called him cad.

Deathwatch and Beadle struggled a little more at Toad's wrists before turning to his feet and discovering, to their embarrassment, that the rack was much too long for its victim.

"'E's too short, sir, and in consequence even if he 'olds on wiv 'is hands one end 'is feet cannot be attached at the other end, *sir!*"

While they were debating the matter, Toad sat up and wandered off to have a closer look at some of the other appliances, which drew even more admiring remarks from the crowd. Some of the ladies who had fainted now began to give him coy and admiring glances. One asked for his autograph, which he gave with a flourish.

"My Lords," said Toad, "may I just say that the Iron Maiden, though it is not quite flattering to my figure and looks a trifle over-large, does offer prongs that overlap and so it might work, though I couldn't be sure till we try it."

"Wrong ordination," said the Parish Clerk.

"I'll waive my right to object," said Toad, "for I am getting hungry and am looking forward to my luncheon, not having eaten very much else but dry crusts of late."

The Judges gave their approval.

Unresisting, and with a last wave to his now admiring audience, Toad was placed inside the Iron Maiden and to cries of "Good Luck!" the spike-filled door was shut upon him.

Terrible cries issued forth, and muffled shouts, and then grim silence.

"'E's done for this time, but 'e put up a good show," said one of the Villagers.

"It cannot be," wept one of the fainting ladies, "he was so brave and did not look like a criminal at all."

"Open up and see what is left inside," said Purposeful.

Deathwatch and Beadle did so and to everybody's astonishment, and to Lord Mallice's evident discomfiture,

Toad stepped out breathing heavily, and took a bow.

"Tight, but not tight enough," said Toad with great aplomb once he had got his breath back. "You tore my suit, I'm afraid, and broke a button, which is why I cried out, and after that I had to hold my breath and keep my tummy in.

"Now don't be downhearted, Mr Deathwatch and Brother Beadle, for this is no ordinary, run-of-the-mill criminal you are dealing with. This is innocence personified. You see before you one who has escaped from tighter spots than this. My name is Toad, Toad of Toad Hall, and I defy your instruments to cause me discomfort, but I will sue you personally if they cause further damage to my apparel!"

This speech, Toad's first real one, drew applause from the crowd, some of it rapturous, and it was all too plain that the Judges would have to take things in hand if the trial were not to swing in Toad's favour.

The Judge Pitiless stood up and said, "Leave this to me." Then to Deathwatch and Beadle he said, "Put him in that iron cage and swing him over the brazier."

"Braising is not till after strining," warned the Parish Clerk.

"The prisoner has waived his rights in perpetuity," said Pitiless. "Do it."

It would have been better if Toad had protested, as he had every right to do. But he was enjoying himself now and, convinced of his own invincibility, he offered no resistance. He climbed into the cage of his own free will, closed the door behind him and even helped to hold the padlock as the masked duo fastened it.

They attached a rope that was already threaded through a pulley in the beams above and hoisted Toad aloft, from where he began to declaim his own brilliance and excellence, and explained that as a Toad he was not made as others were, so none should attempt any of his feats in the privacy of their own homes where help might not be at hand.

"In fact, ladies and gentlemen, in fact –"

But now, as he was swung over the brazier and lowered through its rising smoke towards its bright and ready flames, his voice faltered and he observed, "Hang on, this is hot, and getting hotter. In fact, it is really very hot – rather *too* hot in my opinion, and my shoes – why, my shoes are beginning to burn! I say, you chaps, could you perhaps – please could you – I mean – *help!*"

Up till this moment in the proceedings, by virtue of his silence and stillness, and because his box remained in shadow, His Royal Highness the Prince had said nothing. Now, however, he intervened, though few saw him do so. He signalled to one of the court officials and passed a note from the box which he indicated should be taken up to a certain gentleman on the upper row.

The gentleman he pointed at was Mole

Even as Toad's cries became more outraged and, it must be said, more desperate, and the rich odours of burning leather and singeing Harris tweed began to fill the Court Room, Mole received the note, read it, looked up in amazement and not a little glee and indicated to the Rat and the Otter where the note had come from.

Then the Mole leapt to his feet and cried, "On behalf of the accused, I demand compurgation and the wager of law!"

Once before the Judges had appeared surprised; this time they were utterly dumbfounded.

"Compurgation?" spluttered Purposeful.

"Wager of law?" gasped Pitiless.

"It does seem so, I fear," concluded the Judge Perspicacious. "Bring him down!"

Deathwatch and Beadle duly swung the perspiring Toad away from the brazier and back down to ground level.

"Mr Toad," said Purposeful, "kindly stop smouldering and return to the dock."

Toad did so.

"There has been a plea on your behalf for compurgation, which is to say –"

"Which is to say," said the Parish Clerk, "that if twelve good men and true herein testify by shouting 'Aye' to your character then you will be let off scot-free and the chief witness tried in your place."

"But – but –!" expostulated Mrs Ffleshe in horror.

"My dearest," said Lord Mallice with cunning mien, "be of good cheer, for if twelve good men and true do *not* testify and only eleven or ten or nine come forward then Mr Toad shall be instantly tined, and those oath-takers likewise, is that not so, Parish Clerk?"

"It is," said the Parish Clerk, turning up ancient statute to confirm the point.

"So," said the Judge Pitiless, "let those who would

testify to the condemned's character raise their right hand and call out 'Aye'."

Six hands went up immediately, comprising the entire Action Committee from the Village, and the gentleman who had called Toad a cad and bounder but had come to admire him. Each in turn cried "Aye!"

"Six thus far," said Pitiless. "Six more are needed."

Two more hands went up; two more "Ayes" were heard.

"Four short," said Pitiless.

A grim silence fell upon the crowd.

After a further pause Lord Mallice, looking smug, said, "My Lords, it is perfectly obvious –"

"Aye!" called a voice from the crowd.

It was the Otter.

And then "Aye!" and "Aye!"

It was Ratty and Mole.

"One more is needed," said the Parish Clerk, "which is to say fewer than two but more than none."

Even his normally calm voice showed excitement, and the crowd looked about to see if there were any takers.

"My Lords," said Lord Mallice once again, "it seems that –"

"Aye!"

It was the twelfth and last, and it brought a gasp from the crowd that mixed relief and disappointment in equal measure. And then astonishment.

For that last "Aye!" came from the Prince Himself who now rose up so that his face could finally be seen.

It was no prince that they saw.

It was Mr Badger of the Wild Wood, he who had told the Mole what to do in Toad's moment of mortal danger.

"Aye!" growled the Badger once again, staring his challenge at Lord Mallice.

"O My Lord," cried Mrs Ffleshe, "it seems that I am undone and shall be twined or twanged or whatever it is."

"Not so, dearest madam," said Lord Mallice, "for I shall lodge an appeal which cannot be denied and it will not be heard for an eternity. Put your trust in me and I shall be your Lord."

Mrs Ffleshe sighed and murmured, almost gently, that she had done so in spirit long since.

"But in any case, My Lords," continued the ever resourceful Mallice, "I greatly fear that one of these twelve compurgators is ineligible and so the quorum is not met!"

A gasp, and the crowd followed the direction of his pointing finger and seeing through his poor disguise now recognised Mr Mole of Mole End.

"That gentleman is Mr Mole and he is a fugitive from justice and can hardly testify to his co-defendant's character. Mr Toad has had his chance and only eleven good men and true have come forward – and in fact that number may be reduced to ten for Mr Badger may well be arraigned for impersonating His Royal Highness the –"

"Enough! I have heard enough!"

This was a new voice, and it came not from the Bench, nor from the crowd. Not from the witnesses for the prosecution, nor from Toad.

Rather, it came from that gentleman whom all had assumed to be the servant of the one they had believed to be the Prince. It came from the small gentleman who sat next to Badger in the Royal Box.

"It is enough, I say!"

"And who, sir, are you to so interrupt the Court's proceedings?" cried all three Judges, accompanied by Lord Mallice.

"I might ask the same of *you,* sir, but I will not!" said the stranger with some asperity, rising with difficulty and leaning on Badger's arm as he came into the light. "Instead, I'll answer your question with as much politeness as is left in me after being forced to witness such a travesty of justice against Mr Toad of Toad Hall!"

His stature, though small, held great authority; his voice, though quiet, carried great force.

"Groat's my name," said he, "and wasting time and words is not my game. Call me Lord of this Manor if you will or if you won't, it don't make any difference, for that's what I am whether you like it or not. Now, if I am not very much mistaken – and I am *not* – it is I who have jurisdiction over this Court and not you, My

Lords. I therefore find the defendant not guilty and pronounce that he is free to leave this Court forthwith!"

All the ladies in the crowd, including even Mrs Ffleshe, fainted there and then.

Only one gentleman fainted, and that was Toad.

He looked right, he looked left, he looked skyward and he looked down, and then with nowhere else to look and stuck for any word to say, he swooned into the trusty arms of Deathwatch and his colleague, Beadle.

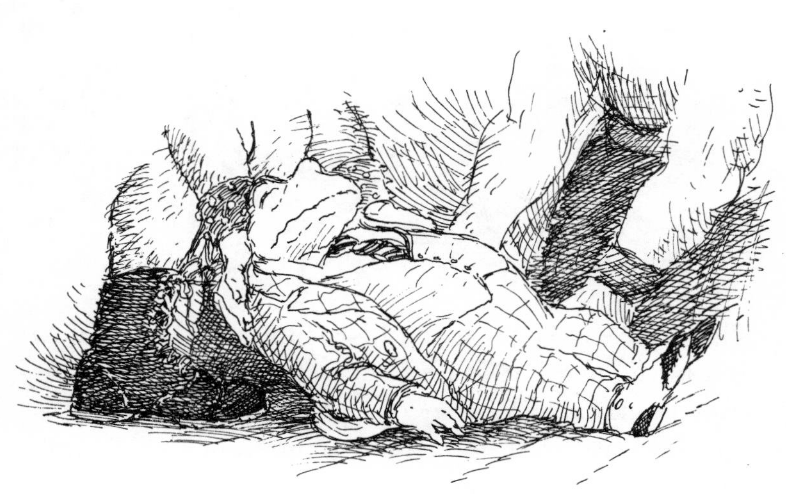

· XII ·
Twelfth Night

The moment Groat made his astonishing appearance and brought the trial of Toad to a summary end, the crowd erupted in a frenzy of clapping and cheering.

In no time at all the heroes of the hour (which is to say Toad, Mole, Badger, Ratty and Otter, and, most reluctant of all, Uncle Groat) were hoisted on the shoulders of the Village menfolk and transported outside on to the bridge, to a rapturous reception and a good many speeches.

The weather being chilly, and the heroes and their many supporters being thirsty, they very soon made their way to the Public House to enjoy free beer, at the expense of Toad, and much laughter and jollity, at the expense of nobody.

Most of the villains of the piece, which is to say the three Judges Perspicacious, Purposeful and especially Pitiless, as well as all the weasels and stoats in the vicinity and Mrs Ffleshe's guests, beat a hasty retreat. The Judges went back to Town as fast as their carriages would carry them, and the Wild Wooders fled to the one place they could not be easily pursued, which is to say the Wild Wood.

Mrs Ffleshe and Lord Mallice, however, lingered in the Court House, though not from any fear that if they went outside a medieval form of public justice might be meted out upon them. Neither was temperamentally inclined to such feelings of cowardice, and if confronted by the mob might very easily have faced it down.

No, there was a more potent reason why they stayed behind, which had to do with an emotion very different from fear.

It had not been lost on some in the crowd that in the dramatic exchanges between the Prosecuting Counsel and his chief witness there had been a certain expression of something more than mutual admiration.

Once the Court Room had emptied of its crowd, Lord Mallice found himself alone at last with Mrs Ffleshe with only the rack between them.

"O madam," said he, "you were magnificent in all."

"Lord," said she, "I swoon to think of the questions you put, and your pauses between – so masterful, so proud, so eloquent in their brutal simplicity."

"Let us speak not of me, Mrs Ffleshe, but thee," said he, advancing upon her by way of the mangler and the thumbscrews.

"You stand accused, madam, of being unutterably ideal, how do you plead?"

"My Lord, if I am guilty it is because you have made me so. Prosecute me, cross-examine me, and when you have done, sentence me as you will!"

"To marriage, madam, that is my sentence."

"To matrimony, My Lord, that is my answer!"

It may be a matter of surprise to some that such as these should be able to wrest from their adamantine hearts sentiments so gentle and so soft. But these were mortal beings born of mortal parents. Put another way, as a slug has a father and a snake a mother, so Mrs Ffleshe and Lord Mallice had parents once, and were young and soft and not to be utterly reviled.

But perhaps, after all, the spirit of Christmas understood better than any human being could that the best way of ridding the earth of tyrants is to make them experience love.

It may well be that these private sentiments so boldly expressed in what they thought was privacy saved the Parish Clerk from a wretched fate. For throughout their dialogue he had stood unseen at the top of the steps that led to that doleful door through which the condemned ought by rights to have finally gone but had not. In his hand was an ancient key, and before him the portal he had just unlocked, and below him the death-dealing torrent into which he was about to jump following the shameful debacle in his Court.

Then he had heard that word "matrimony" and he remembered that in the midst of death is life, and in life continuing duty.

"Lord and madam," said he, turning, "in this your hour of need I am the one to plight you, for I am Registrar of Births (none today), Deaths (several very nearly, none finally) and Marriages (yours, hopefully). I am still wearing my black robe, I have my wig to hand, and beneath that Bench is the Book of Record."

"You can marry us immediately?" said Mrs Ffleshe with something of her normal sharpness.

"Immediately, yes," said the Parish Clerk. "Tomorrow possibly, after that with difficulty, for I may be retiring."

"So you can marry us here and now?" said Lord Mallice.

"Immediately, yes," said the Clerk.

"Don't we need witnesses?"

"History shall be your witness," said he, "but if you want real ones I shall summon Mr Deathwatch and Mr Beadle. They can sign the book."

"What about the ring?" asked Mrs Ffleshe, as women often will.

"Plenty of those," said the Parish Clerk, "in the Court House safe."

He fetched a boxful of rings of all shapes and sizes.

"Whose are these?" enquired Mrs Ffleshe in some surprise.

"The rings of the past condemned and now deceased," said the Parish Clerk. "Now say after me..."

When, later that afternoon, the celebrations were well done – *very* well done – Uncle Groat, who was feeling a little tired, asked that they might all return to Toad Hall, there to recover a little, and talk and celebrate more peaceably.

He was all the more anxious to get to Toad Hall as he had not had time even to pause after his hasty journey from the north with the Badger and Miss Bugle. From their conversations on the journey south he and the Badger had formed a healthy respect for each other. Groat had explained very fully his impatience with life at the River Bank before he left it, and his desire to forge his own path through life, which he had done better and more successfully than most. For his part, the Badger left him in no doubt that a small effort now, and a big-hearted gesture, would make all the difference to the life of Toad, of the River Bank and of them all. Which Groat had come to see was true.

He had been reluctant to show his face in Court, since, unusually for a member of his family, he preferred to stay in the background. But he had seen the way things were going and that his intervention was needed if his nephew were not to suffer trials that might prove terminal, and so he had finally acted.

But enough was enough, and now he wanted to cede the Lordship to Toad and go back to peaceful retirement. Before that he proposed to extract a promise from Toad that the office would not be abused, nor even often used.

"Rather," said he, "let a veil of silence fall over this painful incident in which the Toad family was so nearly humiliated and only survived by a show of bravado by you, and a display of timeliness by myself, upon which qualities you have built your reputation and I my fortune. Shall we now agree to put these twelve days behind us, and the memory of Nanny Fowle and Mrs Ffleshe as well, and never speak of them again?"

Solemnly, on the road between the Village and Toad Hall, Toad did so, and so did all the other River Bankers. They shook hands upon it, and kept that promise to their dying day.

By the time they reached Toad Hall, the Badger could see that Groat was tired and in need of rest. Badger was sensible as well of Groat's natural desire to re-discover the place of his birth and early years without others impinging themselves, excepting Toad, who could, and would, impinge all he liked, for he was family.

"Come on, Uncle," said Toad jovially when they reached the front door of Toad Hall once more, "let's see if you can remember where Pater kept the champagne!"

As they ascended the steps the front door opened and out came Miss Bugle.

"Sirs!" she cried. "O, sirs! I never thought I would see Mr Groat and Mr Toad together at Toad Hall! Welcome back, welcome back!"

The others left them then, with promises that on the morrow, and perhaps in the days thereafter too, they would visit frequently and make up for time lost in the Village Gaol.

"O my," said the Mole as they turned back out of the entrance to Toad Hall, "I have just realised that it is Twelfth Night, and dusk is nearly upon us! Now, Badger and Ratty, and Otter too, did you not say you would come to Mole End and be my guests?"

"We did indeed," said the Rat. "Did we not, you fellows?"

Badger and Otter nodded their agreement.

"Well then," said the Mole, "you had better hurry along with me, for time is running out and there is much to do if we are to enjoy ourselves before the decorations must all come down. Mole End has been neglected these twelve days past."

Which was true, for even after he had escaped from the Village Gaol the Rat and the Otter had judged it imprudent for Mole to go back home.

"It'll be under observation by the weasels and stoats and you'll be needed to help when Toad is tried," the ever practical Rat had said – and how right he had been!

"Mind you, it won't take me long to light a fire, though getting the range warm enough for cooking may take a little while," said the Mole as they cut across the fields.

"O dear, I fear Mole End will *not* be as welcoming as it would have been on Christmas Day. But then it really doesn't matter because if we all muck in together we'll have everything ship-shape and in working order in no time at all, as you would put it, Ratty!"

Mole chattered on happily, making excuses one moment and proclaiming his pleasure the next. While Badger, Otter and Rat said once if not a hundred times that all that mattered to them was that he was happy in his home, and content to see them there.

"O I am, I mean I shall be, because nowadays, don't you see, it is you three fellows, along with Toad, who are all the family that I have. I see that now, and I have come to accept that I will never again – not ever – I shall never –"

As they came in sight of Mole End itself, Mole's chatter suddenly stopped, and his voice faded to silence; and well it might.

For his little home was not dark and cold, unlit and unwelcoming. Why, there was candlelight at his windows, and a freshly decorated wreath upon his door! From the chimney there issued smoke that betokened a fire as bright and cheerful as the Mole had often said Twelfth Night fires *should* be.

"But I do not understand," he whispered in astonishment. "I mean to say, there is no one who – there is surely no one now – I mean – I mean –"

He turned from one to the other, uncertain what to say and not daring to go on.

"It's your home, Mole, you lead the way," commanded the Rat with a twinkle in his eye.

"O but I dare not even think what I want to hope!" cried the Mole.

"Then you had better hope what you cannot think!" responded the Rat with a laugh. "Off you go, Mole, and *in* you go –"

They watched as the Mole approached his home ahead of them. They saw him stop as a curtain twitched and a face looked out. It was female, it was Mole-like, and Mole could not believe his eyes.

He approached a little more and he was but three steps away when his front door opened and the light of festive welcome flooded forth in which, bright and cheerful, and her eyes as full of tears as Mole's own, his beloved sister stood.

"O Mole!" she cried.

"O –" he whispered brokenly as he went to her and she took him gently in her arms, "O my!"

Rarely, perhaps never, was there a Twelfth Night celebration like the one that evening at Mole End. Such stories to be told and heard; such adventures to be relived; such emotions to be shared!

First Mole heard how Miss Bugle had insisted, absolutely insisted, that the Badger and she take time to find the Mole's sister on their way north to visit Uncle Groat.

Then he heard that not only had they found her but better still it was Miss Bugle who persuaded Groat where his duty lay, for, she told him, "What use is wealth if it does not serve your family and friends before yourself? No use at all! Your brother Toad Senior said so many times!"

Mole's sister then listened to the story of how he had been incarcerated, how he had escaped, and how Toad had been tried and acquitted.

Finally, the Badger and the others heard how she and the Mole had spent their childhood years, especially at festive times.

"My, was she a home-maker, was she a cook!" they exclaimed concerning their mother.

"Yet there are some things you did even better," said the Mole, "such as, for example, mince pies. Here, have some more, you fellows, for I'm sure you'll never taste better than these!"

"That reminds me, Mole," said his sister, pulling a piece of paper from her apron pocket, "here is a belated Christmas gift."

The Mole looked at it, read it, folded it and tucked it into his jacket pocket.

"What is it?" asked the Badger.

"The recipe for these mince pies!" said the smiling Mole. "Which reminds *me*..."

He went to his larder and emerged a moment later with a jar of candied angelica. As he handed it round, and they exclaimed at its perfection, he told his sister, "And as promised, in return *you* shall have my recipe for angelica."

So did brother and sister, and friends as well, see that Twelfth Night through.

As midnight approached, they all helped the Mole take down the decorations as tradition demanded they must. Then Mole and his sister walked down the little lane to his crab-apple tree, and they wassailed its health for the coming year.

Later, back in front of the fire, the Mole gave them each a pot of his crab-apple jelly, blushed with blackberries, made to a recipe his mother had taught him. Then they continued to talk till midnight came and with it the end of the festive season.

Finally, with great reluctance, Badger, Ratty and Otter bade their farewells to as happy a Mole as ever lived. They stood briefly together upon his threshold and made their wishes for the coming of Spring, of Summer and of Autumn that joys might be many, and fruits plentiful.

"Goodbye for now, you fellows," he called softly after them, "and may your every wish come true!"

THE END

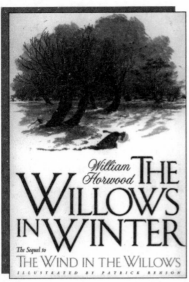

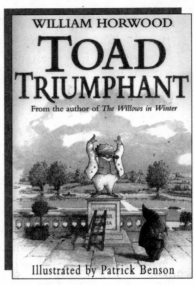

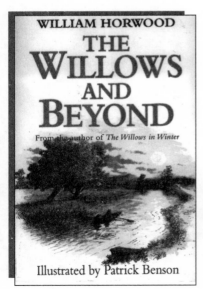